Waiting for Time to Tell

Book Three of The Thomas Hall Series

Beth Sorensen

Contents

A Note from The Author   V

1. Chapter One   1

2. Chapter Two   3

3. Chapter Three   11

4. Chapter Four   21

5. Chapter Five   33

6. Chapter Six   45

7. Chapter Seven   53

8. Chapter Eight   61

9. Chapter Nine   67

10. Chapter Ten   75

11. Chapter Eleven   85

12. Chapter Twelve   93

13. Chapter Thirteen   103

14. Chapter Fourteen   117

15. Chapter Fifteen   129

16. Chapter Sixteen   135

17. Chapter Seventeen   141

18. Chapter Eighteen   153

19. Chapter Nineteen   167

20. Chapter Twenty   177

21. Chapter Twenty-One   185

22. Chapter Twenty-Two   191

23. Chapter Twenty-Three   205

24. Chapter Twenty-Four   213

25. Chapter Twenty-Five   225

26. Chapter Twenty-Six   233

27. Chapter Twenty-Seven   243

28. Chapter Twenty-Eight   253

29. Chapter Twenty-Nine   259

30. Chapter Thirty   267

31. Epilogue   279

A Note from The Author

It has been over a decade since *Crush at Thomas Hall* and *Divorcing a Dead Man* were released for the first time. A lot has changed in the world since then, both in society and with technology. However, only five months have passed within the world of Thomas Hall since the end of *Divorcing a Dead Man* and the beginning of this novel, *Waiting for Time to Tell*. As the author, I have made the decision to use modern technology and societal norms as they exist today. This may create a few discrepancies between the first two novels and this, the third novel of The Thomas Hall Series. I hope you enjoy this final installment of the series and will be happy to know that something new is currently in the works.

Happy Reading!

Beth Sorensen

October 2022

<h1 style="text-align:center">Chapter One</h1>

I STEPPED INTO THE steamy shower and let the hot water beat against the back of my head and shoulders. As it did, the tension in my neck subsided slightly. I turned carefully not to let the bandage on my left arm or right temple get wet, opened my eyes, and looked down. When I did, I saw it all. The crimson blood, the bits of skin, brains, and bone fragments previously tangled in my hair and plastered on my body washed down the drain. I felt light-headed and dizzy, so I closed my eyes and leaned against the shower wall until the feeling passed. No wonder the people who converged on Poppy's home left me alone. I must have looked like something out of a horror movie.

I shampooed my hair three times, scrubbing my body between hair washings until my skin was bright pink and raw. Once my senses were overrun with the scent of lilacs and I was certain there was nothing left of the evidence of the nightmare that occurred, I turned the water off and stepped out of the hotel shower.

As I wrapped myself in one of the fluffy, oversized hotel towels, the pile of bloody clothes lay in a messy heap on the bathroom floor, serving as still more evidence of the bloodbath I witnessed. I gathered the clothes from the floor and threw them all in the trash. I could not believe I let myself traipse through Chicago late on a summer night looking like that. I never wanted to see that dress again. It did not matter that it was my husband's favorite. I would never be able to wear it, even if it were possible to remove the stains. The memories would be too heartbreaking. I tossed the shoes in the trash bin on top of the dress as well. Those stilettos hurt my feet every time I wore them.

I wiped the steam from the mirror and looked at myself. Pale skin accentuated the dark circles residing under my eyes. Even my round-cheeked face looked sunken in. I now had confirmation of something I had begun to suspect. Now that I knew what I knew and had seen what I'd seen, my life would never be the same. I stretched out across the bed, still wrapped in a towel, and thought about everything that occurred in such a short period of time.

Chapter Two

Dinner with Poppy and Vivian at the main house of Thomas Hall was always entertaining. The winery I ran not only had gorgeous vineyards but was the property upon which my husband's family's homes were built. The main house was Vivian's, the family matriarch, and more often than not of late, I found myself eating dinner at her house and not at the home where I resided. I probably should say where my husband and I resided, but that would require him to be home.

When Edward and I met, we started a whirlwind love affair that included moving in together and getting married, all within three months. From the beginning, I knew that we would not be together every night. His work was in Washington D.C. and my life quickly became about his family's winery an hour south of the Capital near Willow Creek, Virginia. Edward had come home less and less over the course of the last few months until he was only there one night a week.

I sat silently, listening as the senior lovebirds regaled me with their latest adventure as a member of the kitchen staff served dark chocolate mousse with cherries and whipped cream for dessert.

Vivian Baker, my mother-in-law, and Poppy Scarpelli, the grandfather of my late husband, were introduced just before the holiday season and were officially a couple by the time the new year began. Many people in town felt Vivian's mourning of her late husband had been far too short. The reality though was that Vivian did not like being alone and found my beloved grandfather excellent company. Her children were not certain about their mother jumping into another relationship either, especially with Chicago's notorious mob boss. But after seeing her happiness and getting to know Poppy better, they had no objections.

The two had just returned from Niagara Falls. They had chosen the destination because neither had ever been and thought it would be fun.

"... and that's how we ended up walking into the lobby of the hotel soaking wet," Vivian said as she finished her story.

I smiled. Normally, a story that ended like that, and included the two of them, would have me laughing until tears streamed down my face. However, even the most joyful things in my life were diluted as of late. Vivian looked at Poppy and then me.

"Okay, Cassandra. What's going on?" Vivian asked.

"What do you mean?"

"Why are you so miserable these days? We both see it."

"Miserable seems a bit excessive, don't you think?" I asked, although I knew she was right. I stuffed a spoonful of the decadent dessert in my mouth so they would not expect me to continue talking.

"You are most certainly not happy, my dear." As Poppy spoke, his cell phone quietly rang. He looked at the caller ID, shook his head, and stood up from the table. "I am sorry ladies. I need to take this."

We both watched him walk out of the dining room. The dining room was a grand space that most would consider a ballroom. The cherry wood floors were so highly polished that, in the few spaces not covered by large Turkish rugs, the light reflected from the three chandeliers which were equally spaced across the ceiling.

When he was gone, Vivian moved from her usual seat, abandoning her mousse, and sat next to me, taking my hands in hers. She had beautiful, delicate hands and her fresh manicure only enhanced them.

"What's wrong? Talk to me."

I hesitated but found myself telling her the truth. I'd managed to give people dismissive answers to the same question for weeks, but I knew my mother-in-law would not accept any of them.

"I miss your son, that's all." I stared at the floor in the dining room as I answered and punctuated my statement with a loud sigh.

Her son, Edward, and I had been married for five months. In the beginning, our marriage was full of romance, and while my life was usually chaotic, being married to Edward seemed like the most natural thing on earth. He thought so as well. Until a couple of months ago. Something shifted in early March and I had no clue what facilitated it, but it left me longing for a husband I rarely saw.

"When was the last time the two of you spent any time together?"

"When we had Sunday lunch with the two of you before you headed to Niagara Falls."

"My dear, that was a week ago."

"I know, we talk and text, but it's not the same." I hesitated before I continued, whispering the remainder of my thought. "I think he's grown tired of me."

"I doubt that dear. He's just very busy."

"He's always too busy," I said as I licked the last of the chocolate from my spoon and then set it in the dish in which my dessert had been served. "At least too busy for me anymore."

I waited for a response from Vivian, but none ever came. Just a look of concern. It was as if she knew where my mind was going. What I was considering I did not approve of but I was beginning to believe it was my only choice.

"Cassandra," Vivian, seemingly having read my thoughts, stared at me as she spoke, and fear crossed her face for a brief moment. "Please tell me you aren't thinking about leaving my son."

I felt my eyes start to flood with tears and squeezed them shut in an attempt to stop the tears from escaping. "Vivian, what's the point if he's never here?"

Just then, Poppy entered the room looking annoyed and returned to his seat, saving me from having to actually answer Vivian's question. Poppy had not aged since I first met him nearly a decade ago. He had gray, slicked-back hair, bright blue eyes, and was as round as he was tall. As always, he wore a bespoke suit. He had dozens of them which seemed appropriate for the leader of the Scarpelli Crime Family. Today's choice was light gray with a crisp white shirt and purple tie with gray poke-a-dots. With the exception of joy, Poppy liked to keep his emotions hidden so I was more curious than concerned.

"Poppy, is everything okay?" I asked.

"My granddaughter is stirring things up, as usual."

"Which one?" Vivian asked. "You have eight." She included me in that number, just as Poppy always did. Of the eight, I was the only one not related by blood as I was the former wife of his late grandson, Tony Martin. I was the youngest of the grandchildren as well at age twenty-six.

"Your former sister-in-law, Isabella," Poppy said with a chagrinned smile.

"Wait, isn't she in jail?" I asked, confused as to her current whereabouts. It was alarming to me that Isabella, whom many called Izzy, could be out and about, no doubt up to her old tricks of inciting madness and mayhem. She was everything you would expect a mob princess to be, so it was hard to picture the petite, five-foot-tall girl with olive skin, big boobs, long black hair teased within an inch of its life, and a heart-shaped face behind bars. But knowing both her attitude and actions, I was surprised Izzy had not landed there sooner. She was a textbook definition of a Napoleon complex with her domineering personality and explosive temper.

"No. She is out of prison. I probably should have left her there. She is not behaving as a good granddaughter should." He looked at me and smiled. I silently nodded and kindly accepted the compliment.

"Should I even ask why?" Vivian continued with the follow-up questions.

"She's disrupting the organization's structure. Giving contradictory orders to our soldiers after they have been briefed.

"Soldiers?" Vivian asked, slightly confused. Organized crime was not a world she had grown up in. As an adult, I lived on the fringes of it. Never personally involved with any of it, but respectful of the family business. In doing this, I was in turn, treated with respect and kindness by anyone associated with the Scarpelli family. Vivian had taken the same approach, after discussing it with me, which yielded similar results.

"The lower-level associates, my dear." She nodded her head and he continued. "This is not a wise move. The chain of command must be respected."

"Is it appropriate for me to ask what you will do?" In Poppy's world, I was often uncertain whether or not I was overstepping my boundaries, and this case was no exception. Whenever I felt that way, I always asked if it was appropriate to even ask. Poppy liked that and from what I had been told, so did his associates, though I had not met many.

"It is," Poppy replied as he smiled. "However, I am not certain I have an answer yet."

Later that evening, as the sun was just dipping below the horizon, I made my way along the pebbled path that looped within the center of the property and connected all the houses to the production building. The late April breeze was still cool, but warmer weather was definitely in the near future. I did not rush home but enjoyed the breeze pushing the scent of the newly formed grapes towards me. There was no reason to hurry because no one would be there. I would be alone again tonight. It was not too late for me to drive to Washington D.C. but the last time I did that, I spent the evening alone in his apartment, while he was still at the office, and I spent the night on the verge of tears. I hated that place. My husband spent more and more time sleeping there because it was near his office even though the trip from Thomas Hall was only an hour. This was not what I expected when we wed and while I kicked pebbles as I walked, I contemplated whether my decision to marry Edward had been a wise one.

My eyes popped open and I sprung into a sitting position. The clock on the bedside table read two twenty-four. The terror I awoke to rolled over me in waves. Beads of sweat coated my hairline slowly rolling down my face and neck. This, in combination with the intermittent chills, intensified nausea that rose in my stomach. I could feel my heart racing and hear the blood swishing in my ears. My chest was so tight that I could not breathe either. Fear sucked the oxygen from the room when I tried to inhale. This made my go-to calming technique impossible. Focusing on your breathing does no good when the inability to breathe is part of the issue.

I sat in the center of the bed, silently praying for this feeling to pass. As I did, the room began spinning. I grab ahold of the comforter as if it could steady me. A choking feeling found a way to add itself to my inability to breathe and I was certain I was going to either vomit or pass out. Maybe both.

The symptoms began to subside but as they did, I started to shake. I had experienced both nightmares and panic attacks before, but this was the first time I woke from a nightmare while in the middle of a panic attack.

The nightmare was something different than what I had previously experienced. Usually, it was the memory of a single tragic event in my life. My parents' death, being beaten next to the body of my dead father-in-law, the kidnapping, or any of the monumental dark moments of my life. This time, however, it was a montage of my life. There were family vacations, picnics, my wedding, and my honeymoon. These beautiful moments lulled me into happiness as I slept just before death, destruction, and despair wedged their way between the happy milestones leaving no terrifying moment of my life omitted. It was all strung together in a never-ending loop.

I had never been alone when a panic attack occurred. This was new as it always happened in crowded places. I was still shaking when I laid my head back on the pillow. That night, I cried myself back to sleep.

Chapter Three

I SAT AT MY desk the next morning, enjoying a delicious, but not overly sweet, cake donut and drinking tea, even though I had already eaten breakfast. I was trying to make sense of the financial records from the last quarter and they were not looking as good as I hoped. My office was pretty much unchanged from when its previous owner ran the winery. The massive room was beautifully decorated with spectacular views of the vineyards, an elegant wine tasting bar, and a matching cherry wood desk. Oriental carpets covered the industrial flooring of the production building and a sofa, chairs, side tables, and bar stools filled the room making it feel cozy.

I had gained controlling interest in Thomas Hall Winery after the death of Edward's father, Senior, last autumn. It had been his pet project and had turned itself into a business, but it had never been profitable. Senior had convinced himself that somehow I could figure out how to turn this wonderful money pit into a thriving business. He greatly overestimated my abilities.

I knew nothing about winemaking and even less about running a business. Every single day since taking over had been a learning experience. And this particular day was about to be no different.

I had just popped the last bite of donut in my mouth when Alex, Thomas Hall's winemaster, came into my office and dropped himself onto my sofa. He looked like he should be surfing, not making wine. His shaggy sun-bleached blonde hair and tan skin complimented his good looks and trim physique. He was Edward's half-brother and not much older than I was at twenty-eight. Most people in the wine industry did not take him seriously, but they would. He was smart, talented, and had a long-term plan for his career. Most people in the wine industry were not taking me seriously either. Most days I agreed with them, but I was asked to do a job by a man I respected. I did not want to let my late father-in-law's legacy collapse, so I showed up and gave it everything I could.

As soon as Alex saw my face he said, "You didn't sleep well, did you?"

The dark circles under my eyes had not gone unnoticed by me either. The reflection in my bathroom mirror earlier in the morning revealed everything I had gone through the night before.

"It happens. I'll sleep better tonight." I knew I was being optimistic that my husband would come home from Washington D.C. because I always slept better when we shared a bed.

When I looked up from my paperwork, Alex was not smiling. This was highly unusual for him, especially on a Friday morning.

"How's the morning going?"

"Well..."

"Uh-oh. Nothing good starts with *well* coming out of your mouth."

"We might have a problem. Do you have time to go into the fields this morning?"

"Sure. Can we do it now?"

Alex nodded his head. I stood, set down my mug after one last sip of tea, and grabbed a baseball cap on the way out the door. It did not take long for me to learn that even if I thought I was going to be gone for only a few minutes, that a hat, along with daily sunscreen, were the only thing between me and a sunburnt face when I returned from the vineyard. And occasionally that wasn't even enough.

We could have taken a truck to the proper field but opted to walk instead. The weather made it an irresistible option as it was a beautiful day with a clear, blue sky and a light breeze. Alex and I often preferred to walk. It would give us time to talk about a variety of topics, most of which were either vine or wine related.

"There are vines dying out in one of the far fields."

"What's causing it? Fungus, poor drainage, insect infestation?" I asked.

Alex blew out a deep sigh. "I don't know. I've never seen anything like it. I've already pulled some samples and I'm driving them to the lab at Virginia Tech this afternoon."

We were in a unique position. Geographically, we were less than a day's drive from Virginia Tech's Enology Analytical Services Lab and Alex's roommate his freshman year was one of the lab supervisors. We tried not to take advantage of it, but this was definitely a time to call in favors. Alex could usually figure out when something with the vines was not right. The fact he had no idea what was happening was alarming.

"Should we worry about spread?" When he didn't answer, I looked up at him. It was only then I saw the dark rings under his eyes and the exhaustion in his face. I was fairly certain he had not slept. I put my hand on his bicep and he stopped walking. "Alex, how bad is this?"

"I wish I had a clue. I thought I knew of every disease of vines known to man, but I've never seen anything like this."

Alex started walking again and I realized where we were heading. It was field 782, a grouping of grape vines at the far end of the property. I did not usually make the trek out to this end of the vineyard, but it was my second trip to this field in the last two weeks. The first trip was on a beautiful sunny day when I went wandering around the grounds while pondering the changes occurring within my marriage. That entire afternoon I had not seen a single ailing vine.

As we walked, my cell phone pinged with a text message.

I'm sorry Sweetie, but I won't make it home tonight. I'll see you tomorrow.

While I was not shocked by the text, as it had become the norm, I was shocked by what I saw when we reached marker 782. At least four partial rows of vines were dead. Not ailing, but completely dead.

"What the—?" I couldn't even finish my sentence as I walked over to one of the dead vines, examining it closer. Alex had the crew dig one up earlier and I bent down to take a better look. The vine was completely brown. Fruit, leaves, vine, and roots, all completely devoid of life. "When did this happen?"

"I discovered it yesterday, just before sunset. They're dead. Roots and all." He paused to look around. "Sis, I'm worried. What if it continues to spread?" Both he and my husband's other brother, Henry, had taken up calling me Sis. I liked it. It made me feel even more connected to them.

"What are our options?" I asked.

"Right now, we have two choices. See what Virginia Tech's lab finds or just start digging."

"What's your gut say?"

"Dig. But I always err on the side of caution."

"How many good vines will need to go to stop it?" I was already crunching numbers in my head. Number of vines lost, time to replace and grow vines. I knew I was forgetting something major, but my mind was spinning.

"Conservatively, a two to three good vine margin around the dead plants."

"What kind of loss are we talking about? In financial terms."

Alex sighed as he thought. "Vine loss, replacement vines, loss of fruit, decreased production while new vines grow. Probably $80,000 to $100,000." I had forgotten production loss. The biggest single thing.

"Call the insurance company and talk to our rep. No one else. Thank God we have insurance. Why don't you go ahead and head to the lab. I'll check the fields."

"But Sis, that could take all day."

"Well, your brother just bailed on tonight's plans, so I have the time." Alex had only recently discovered that his father was the late Edward Baker, Sr. My husband, Edward Baker Jr., and his younger brother, Henry, had worked hard to fold him into the family, despite some bad blood between Alex and Henry. Alex was more than willing to leave the past in the past, but Henry was still bitter about the affair Alex had with his late wife, Darla. The whole situation was definitely a work in progress. "I'll walk back to the production building with you, clear my desk, have an early lunch, and then take a full tour of the fields. I'll let you know if I find anything."

"He's bailing on you again?" Alex asked. "This is becoming a regular thing, isn't it?"

"It's fine. I'll get used to it... eventually."

Alex paused and then shook his head as he pulled out his cell phone. "It looks like Edward won't be the only brother bailing on their date. If I'm going to Tech this afternoon, I better let her know."

"Wait? A date? You don't date. You chase, catch, and release."

"Things change, Sis."

"Who's the girl? Anybody I know?"

"You ask a lot of questions, but today you won't get answers." He looked nervous. I wasn't sure what to make of it, so I let it go.

Saturday afternoon, I was sitting at the table in the kitchen with my laptop, scanning the travel websites while window shopping for an escape. It was not the same as getting on a plane and visiting them, but a virtual exploration was the best I could do for now. I was fearful enough of the direction my marriage was headed, that if I went away without Edward, I might not bother to come back.

Lately, I found myself holding my breath as the time grew near for him to arrive. I was anxious he might cancel and feared one day that he would not bother coming home at all. When I heard the door open, I exhaled.

Our home was a beautiful two-bedroom Mediterranean-style villa. Vivian had built all three of her children's homes on the property several years ago for when they stayed at Thomas Hall. Edward rarely used the one built for him until I came to visit the winery in Virginia during Crush season, fell in love, and never left. Henry lived just down the path and Phoebe, the only girl in the family, had a home on the other side of the loop. Our late sister-in-law blew it up in an attempt to kill her last year. She obviously failed but leveled the house in the process. It was being rebuilt and Phoebe intended to move there permanently with her two children once it was complete. Alex lived in the wine master's quarters.

Our home, while Mediterranean on the outside, had more of a Tuscan feel inside. Lots of windows provided natural light and the walls were painted in rich shades of vanilla and chocolate. When I first moved in, it was obvious how little time Edward spent there. While beautiful, it had been void of pictures, books, and mementos that made a house a home. I had carefully curated photos of family and friends, scrapbooks and photo albums of my travels and childhood, video games that Edward loved, and books I could not live without in order to turn the impersonal abode into a loving home.

This time of year, I would have preferred to sit outside on the newly installed patio, but a strong breeze was blowing low, dark clouds towards the winery. It was suffocatingly humid and the smell of rain hung heavy in the air. I suspected a storm would begin any moment. Before I could stand up his arms were wrapped around me and his lips were leaving a trail of soft, wet kisses along my neck. I reached back and ran my fingers through his hair, leaning my head back onto his shoulder and closing my eyes.

My husband was in his late forties but had the energy and attitude of a man half his age. This is probably the reason why neither of us thought the twenty-two-year age gap was an issue when we met. He was tall with gorgeous cocoa-colored eyes, thick dark hair that curled around his ears when he was overdue for a haircut, and the body of a Greek god. I had hit the husband lottery when it came to looks.

Edward froze with his lips still on my neck when he saw my laptop open in front of me, finding the site for Great Adventures Travel Company's Bora Bora Expedition on the screen. "Going somewhere?" He asked, trying to sound lighthearted but instead, his voice fell flat.

I opened my eyes to get a better look at him and smiled. However, he did not return the gesture. He just stared at the screen. I felt the tension build in him as his arms dropped away from me. Edward turned and walked out of the kitchen, so I followed him. He sat on the sofa, resting his elbows on his knees and his head in his hands.

"What's wrong, Honey?"

I sat next to Edward and waited for a reply. He was silent for a moment before lifting his head. He cupped his hand along my jawline. I leaned into it and closed my eyes as I deeply inhaled, catching the scent of Irish Spring soap on his skin.

"Cassandra, I just saw my greatest fear."

"What?" My eyes popped open. "Me planning another vacation? Afraid of a repeat of Greece?" I already knew what he meant. I was fairly certain that he was afraid I was going to leave him. I was fairly certain if things did not change it could become a reality. But I was not ready to say that out loud to him or anyone else.

"I keep thinking I'm going to come home one day and you're going to be gone. You're a nomad in my very constricting world. I know you miss the adventurous traveling you did before we met. I've seen it lately, more than ever. Whether you realize it or not. The jokes about hopping on a plane and running off are starting to sound far too serious. The photo albums from your trips lying on the coffee table and now the online travel site on your computer makes me worry that your departure is inevitable. I can see the wanderlust brewing behind those beautiful emerald eyes." As certain as he sounded, he was wrong. It was not wanderlust brewing behind my eyes. It was loneliness.

"I've told you time and time again that I would never leave you like that. You know I'd really rather have you come with me on my adventures."

"That didn't work out so great the last time we tried it," he said.

"We definitely had different expectations of Santorini. We learned something though. We definitely should do a better job of talking about what we both want before we travel." Edward and I never discussed what we wanted out of a vacation and it did not take long for both of us to realize they were very different things. In retrospect, it made sense. We were very different people.

"Cassie, the hotel did not have glass windows, only shutters, and the only heat was from the fireplace."

"It was a beautiful, ancient, traditional home converted into a hotel. What did you expect?" Edward shrugged his shoulders and I continued. "But the breeze coming off the sea was heavenly and the family that owned the hotel was wonderful." I closed my eyes, smiled, and sighed simultaneously. When I opened them, Edward remained silent, staring at me. I leaned against his chest, wrapped my arms around him, and listened to his heartbeat as if he had just run a fifty-yard dash.

"The trip to Bermuda will be better, I promise." I had gone to a great deal of trouble to make certain that everything would be to Edward's liking. I made certain everything was to his liking and what he expected from a vacation. This trip would be better. It would fix things between us. It had to. I was running out of options.

Chapter Four

I HAD TO DO this. As I walked onto the plane, I took my seat in the first-class cabin and the attendant closed the door behind me. The stale recirculated air immediately made me want for fresh air as I buckled the seatbelt. I was the last person to board the flight and I was alone. Edward had sent me a text.

I'm sorry Sweetie, but I'm stuck in a meeting. I'm not going to make the flight.

I stood at the gate with only moments to decide. Edward and I had planned this trip for months. Where we would go, where we would stay, and what we would do were all a matter of playful banter and discussion. However, this was not the first time he canceled this trip on me either. It was the third. The other times it had been the day before or the morning of the trip. But this time I was standing at the gate.

I did not bother to text him back. Once I was in my seat, I powered off my cell phone and shoved it into my purse. It was a decision with untold consequences, whether I realized it or not at the time.

It had been ages since I had flown on a commercial flight, as we usually traveled by private jet. However, before we moved the trip to these dates, I had donated the use of the jet to Angel Flight for the week. The plane was currently transporting a child to St. Jude's Hospital.

After an uneventful flight, I was certain I would step off the plane into sunny weather with salty air from the breezes off the Atlantic Ocean. Instead, it was dark, dreary, and pouring rain.

"How appropriate," I said sarcastically, even though there was no one with me to listen.

I collected my suitcase and found a taxi to the Rosewood Escapes. It was a beautiful five-star hotel. While this is exactly the kind of place Edward was happy staying at, I preferred small, family-run hotels. They had personality and local flavor. The Rosewood, while outstanding in every way, could have been on any beach, on any island, and I would not have known the difference. And now I was stuck at this resort. Alone.

The last time I was in Bermuda, alone on that occasion as well, I would have never spent a thousand dollars a night on a room. I was more than satisfied with Aunt Nea's Inn. As a matter of fact, Aunt Nea's had been a splurge for me at two hundred a night.

I checked in and was immediately shown to my suite. The rooms were awash in white with azure accents. The canopy bed was modern with clean lines and dark wood. It was obvious that this piece of furniture was the inspiration for the entire suite. The furnishings were only accessories for the multiple windows and sliding glass doors that displayed the breathtaking view, even in terrible weather. I opened the balcony door to let the fresh air in, kicked off my shoes, and laid back on the luxurious down comforter.

The next time I opened my eyes it was six o'clock and someone was knocking on the door. My first thought was of Edward. Had my husband taken a later flight in hopes of salvaging the trip? I was disappointed to discover it was only a bellboy with a chilled bottle of champagne, compliments of the hotel. The Baker name went a long way, even outside of Virginia. It was not the name that I wanted though. It was the man. And he wasn't coming.

Edward and I had reservations for seven o'clock at one of the resort's many restaurants. I saw no need to cancel the reservation. I dressed for dinner, in one of the new dresses I bought for the trip and decided to leave my hair down and free flowing. When I looked in the mirror, I knew Edward would like this dress. I bought it specifically to wear for him. He liked dresses that left my arms bare, my legs showing, and had no complicated buttons or zippers. It had the added bonus of being his favorite color, purple, and showed a fair amount of cleavage. My thoughts wandered to exactly what Edward would think of it. I did not have to ponder long before I knew. He would like it so much that it would end up on the floor, we would end up in bed, and miss our dinner reservation. I shook the thought of his reaction from my head and grabbed my wallet from my purse, sliding the room key card into it.

I had dined alone on numerous occasions and always felt comfortable and found ways to pass the time while waiting for my food. I would read, fill out postcards to send to my uncle or Poppy, and sometimes a person at the next table would strike up a conversation with me. Tonight was different though. The wait between ordering and eating seemed endless at the outdoor restaurant as I watched the moonlight bounce off the Atlantic. In reality, it was the quickest restaurant service I had encountered in quite some time.

After dinner, I was not ready to return to my room. I took off my shoes and walked along the beach, letting my feet feel the still damp pink sand between my toes. As I did, I watched as other couples walked in the sand arm in arm. I wished for that this weekend. Not only that, but I planned on it. A wave of sadness crashed over me and after an hour of aimless roaming in the sand, I headed toward the hotel whose light illuminated the way back. I was in the lobby in less than an hour and headed up to my room. This was not the weekend I had intended it to be. Four days of sun, sand, and Edward. Unfortunately, day one only consisted of sand.

The sunlight pouring through the windows woke me the next morning. I rolled over and stretched out my arm, expecting to find Edward. When I only found linen sheets and down pillows, I opened my eyes to find myself alone, missing my husband, and remembering the previous day's events. I shook the sadness from my mind and wiped away a rouge tear.

I called for room service and while I waited, I dug my black one-piece bathing suit, a sundress that doubled as a cover-up, and sunscreen from my suitcase along with a wide-brimmed straw-colored sunhat. My food arrived quickly and an hour later, I was sitting under an umbrella, freshly coated in sunscreen, in a lounge chair on the pink sand beaches of Bermuda with the latest Deborah Harkness novel in hand.

The weather was absolute perfection for a day at the beach. It was actually a bit warmer than normal for the beginning of May in Bermuda. The temperature hovered around eighty degrees and a light breeze blew a few small fluffy clouds across the sky. I put my book on the arm of my chair, about to go in search of a drink when a cabana boy stopped in front of me with a drink in his hand.

"Ma'am, this is from the two gentlemen at the bar." He pointed towards a beachside bar where two tall, blond, tan men sat. They raised their glasses and nodded. I took the drink from the young man and then paused. What was I supposed to do now? No one had ever bought me a drink before. I guessed that I should thank them.

I walked to the bar drink in hand, and as I did, I noticed they were looking at my body. The whole scene was foreign to me. They introduced themselves and they offered me the stool between them. They were trying to look impressive with their expensive watches and designer sunglasses. Their names went in one of my ears and out the other.

"So, what do the two of you do for a living?" I asked.

"We own an alcohol distribution company on the East Coast. We're here trying to pick up some new accounts."

"Have you ever heard of a winery called Thomas Hall?"

"Yeah, isn't it a pretty small winery? We usually work with larger vendors. They have beautiful wine though." The previously silent one of the pair said politely.

I sat, trying to decide what to do next. I knew these guys were flirting with me and I really wanted to talk shop. After some thought though, I came to the realization it would be inappropriate to continue this attempted social interaction. They wanted things that weren't going to happen with me. I stood and looked back and forth between the two men.

"Well, if you ever decide you're interested in them, call me."

"I'm sorry, but who are you?"

"Cassandra Baker, the owner of Thomas Hall Winery." I watched as both men's jaws drop. I turned, leaving my now empty drink on the bar. I knew they were watching me walk away. I could feel their eyes on me.

"That's Edward Baker's wife?" One said to the other.

"I guess so. I knew she was younger than him but damn. She could be his daughter." I grumbled but kept walking.

"Why do the billionaires always get the most beautiful women?"

"Because they can."

I went back to my chair and read until I had finished my book. I decided it was time for a late lunch. The two men who had bought me a drink were chatting with a beautiful redhead in her mid-thirties, closer to the age of the men. I smiled at them as I returned to my room where I showered and changed before heading into the island's capital, Hamilton, to find both lunch and an adventure. As usual, no matter how much sunscreen I put on, my skin was pink and my shoulders were already forming small blisters. I always struggled with avoiding sunburns at the beach and failed, yet again.

After an amazing salad full of seafood and fresh spinach, I found myself roaming the shopping district. I rarely shopped for anything more than postcards but I promised Brian's girls and my niece and nephew presents upon returning from this trip. I did not remember it being so crowded the last time I was here. Only tourists would be in this area and I felt as if we were packed like sardines. Many people were still in bathing suits with shorts and t-shirts worn over them and the air hung heavy with the coconut scent of suntan lotion. Usually, the scent invoked a peaceful joy within me but today it left me feeling slightly nauseous.

I was walking down by the docks when a cruise ship came into port. Group after group of people descended onto the dock, leaving me overwhelmed. It would be so easy for someone to abduct me here. No one would notice and it would be days before anyone knew that something happened to me. As this thought raced through my head, someone bumped into me with enough force that I stumbled. That's when I felt a pair of hands on my waist. I looked up to see an Italian gentleman in his early fifties. Dark hair, olive skin, and piercing eyes looked back at me as he smiled. For a moment I saw my late husband staring back at me and thought I was going to faint. As soon as I was on my feet, I ran from the man as he began to speak. Even though my head was spinning, I ran until I reached a small park, where I was able to finally escape the hoard of travelers. I found a bench and sat, now covered in sweat, for well over half an hour until I slowed my racing heart.

When I felt like I could breathe again, I made my way down a side street and found a wine shop. I made my way inside the air-conditioned, one-room shop and took a moment to enjoy the cool air before roaming through the aisles. A loud crash of glass behind me caused me to jump. I turned to see a broken bottle of red wine that was accidentally dropped by an older gentleman. You would have thought the sound of the bottle breaking would startle me into a panic. This was not the case. As I looked at the floor of the shop, I watched as the crimson liquid spread into a larger and larger pool. And for a fleeting moment, I was in Thomas Hall's wine cellar discovering the body of my late father-in-law. His face was as clear in my head as it was the morning I met him. It was then I began to hyperventilate. It took mere seconds before I began to shake and chills ran through me. I raced from the shop gasping for air and hailed the first available taxi.

I had never experienced two panic attacks in one day. I wondered if they would have happened if Edward had traveled with me. And if they had, what he would think? I had yet to tell him about them. Originally, I did not want him to worry and I was certain they would pass. But now, five months later, they weren't getting better. They were getting worse.

By the time I returned to my room at Rosewood it was late in the afternoon. I sat on the balcony, drank the champagne delivered the night before, and thought about recent events over the last twelve months. Surprisingly, I remarried although I never thought I would see that day happen.

The last year had not been without its tragedies though. Travel usually helped me forget about all the things that had gone wrong in my life. At least it had worked when I last roamed like a gypsy around the world. It was not working this time.

My kidnapping just prior to marrying Edward by my now late husband rattled me more than I would admit. Tony, my first husband, planned to extort millions from Edward in the promise of my return. His true intention was to put my organs on the black market, auctioned off to the highest bidder. Tony's efforts were thwarted though when he died from being poisoned. My life seemed to be full of events like these, but the kidnapping was a breaking point for me. As much as I wanted to make it disappear, the kidnapping had taken root in my brain in a way that no travel was going to fix. If anything, the crowds encountered in town only seemed to make things worse.

I sat, in deep thought, for who knows how long, trying to come to terms with what I thought I knew about travel, marriage, and my own ability to cope with life. Things were changing. I was not certain if I liked it or not, but I needed to adapt. The more I thought about it, the thing changing the most was me. However, I lacked the skills to verbalize it all, especially where my husband was concerned.

When I stood up, it was dark outside and the moon was once again leaving the surface of the ocean brightly lit along the shore. I knew Bermuda was not going to fix my feelings about the kidnapping. It was not going to fix the problems with my marriage either. Now though, I knew what I was going to do next.

By the time the sun rose, I was already at the airport. There was no need to continue this trip alone. I was not the same person I was a year ago and this trip was not the same trip I had taken then. Not so terribly long ago I had been accused, and rightfully so, of not traveling but running. I knew running wasn't going to work anymore because I had run only to discover that everything followed me. Now that I learned my lesson, it was time to go home.

I was sitting at the gate waiting for boarding to begin when I realized my phone had not made a sound the entire trip. I fished it out of my bag, only to discover it was off. My first thought was that I had forgotten to charge it. Then I remembered turning it off when I boarded the outbound flight. I powered the phone on and it was immediately obvious people were trying to reach me. Twenty-seven voicemails, forty-two missed calls, and thirty-one texts.

"This isn't going to be pretty," I mumbled to myself.

I looked at the missed calls first. Edward, of course, had been the majority of those calls. His assistant, my assistant, my brother-in-law, mother-in-law, and two of my best friends also called, no doubt in search of me.

The texts were, as I expected, not pretty. Again, most were from Edward. They started fairly simple.

I'm sorry I missed the flight. I promise I'll be home early tonight. We'll go out to dinner.

They escalated with every text. From apologetic to angry to panicked to remorseful. These emotions ran through multiple texts and I heard the tone of his voice as I read each line.

I know you're mad. Guilt. *Can we talk about this?* Apologetic. *Where are you?* Frustrated. *DAMN IT, CASSIE! ANSWER YOUR PHONE.* Angry. *I just need to know you're safe.* Panicked. *Please stop shutting me out.* Remorseful.

He was not the only person who left texts. My best friend, Brian, left them too.

Edward just called me. He's in a panic. Call him. If you don't want to talk to him, call me. He just wants to know you're safe. And so do I.

My assistant, Libby-Mae, was more pragmatic.

Mr. Baker just called. He's trying to find you. I thought y'all were leaving for Bermuda today? Mr. Baker just told me about missing the flight. I told him you probably got on the plane without him. PLEASE CHECK IN WITH ME. Your husband is driving me crazy!

I read through all the texts and was just about to dive into the voicemails when they started boarding the flight. I had time for one text. I sent it to Edward.

I'm on my way home. Should be at Thomas Hall by mid-afternoon. I'll call you when I get there.

I knew I was going to be in the doghouse with my husband, probably his whole family, and some of my friends as well. Regardless, I knew without a doubt I had done the right thing. I learned what I needed to know. It was time to stop running and face my life. As I grabbed my carry-on bag, I whispered to myself, "I had to do this".

Chapter Five

When the plane landed in Washington D.C., I took a deep breath as soon as I exited, my body begging for fresh air after four hours on a plane. I collected my suitcase and made my way through customs. The next stop would be securing a car and driver to get me home.

When I exited the secure area though, I found the face of my husband staring back at me. I had never seen him as stone-faced as he was at that moment. No expression, no movement, no smile. I could not believe that he was reacting like this after he was the one who deserted me at the airport Friday morning. I was trying to be polite when I texted him about my return. I had no clue this was the response I would receive.

Edward said nothing and made no move to embrace me as I walked toward him so I kept walking. We were both behaving in ways we never had before and the entire scenario felt foreign to me. He turned and watched for a moment as I walked past him. I really wanted to tell him to bite me as I walked by but was too polite to do so. Edward raced to catch up with me and gently tried to take my luggage but I did not stop moving. I walked out the door and our driver met me, taking my suitcase and carry-on after opening the door. The driver quickly took my bags to the trunk. As he did, Edward got into the car and slammed the door behind him. He wasted no time putting the screen up between us and the driver. As I waited for him to say something, the silence was deafening. After about three minutes, I could not stand it any longer.

"What do you want me to say? I got on the flight. I had to."

"Had to? What the hell do you mean you had to?"

"I needed to figure some things out. Some things I couldn't do here."

"And this figuring something out required being completely out of touch?" There was the real problem. He did not care that I went without him. And to be honest, it hurt more than I thought it would. He did care that he did not know exactly where I was or what I was doing. In his mind, I vanished from the face of the earth leaving him with zero control.

This was the biggest problem that had surfaced so far in our marriage. Edward could not control me and it drove him crazy. My husband was a control freak and everyone knew it, including him. I was okay with it most of the time, but I knew he would not believe what I was about to tell him, even though it was the truth.

"I turned my phone off for the outbound flight and forgot to turn it back on." I braced myself for his reaction and was right to do so.

"For three days?!" He shouted, finally allowing emotion to enter his voice and expression. "Don't lie to me, Cassandra. There is no way you forgot to turn it on the entire trip."

Unlike most people, my phone was not an extension of myself. At one time it was a security blanket for me. Now, however, I didn't feel the need to have it with me constantly. Having nothing to hide, I fished my phone out of my bag and pitched it at him. He had accused me of lying to him and my mood rapidly shifted. I took deep breaths in an effort to quell my anger.

He opened my phone and started flipping through it. As he did, I grabbed a Coke from the cooler and sipped it, allowing the sweet bubbles to land on my tongue and the back of my throat. As Edward looked, he found no sent texts, no read emails, no selfies, no internet searches, or any other sign I had touched my phone since Friday morning. "Hmm."

"Hmm. What?" I responded, trying, and failing, to contain my annoyance with him.

"I guess it was off. I'm sure you can imagine what I thought." Edward's voice was calmer, but agitation still clung to his words.

I sighed, took another sip of my drink, and looked toward the sunroof of the car before closing my eyes.

"At this point Edward, I have no idea what you thought. You just accused me of lying to you so I am guessing it could be any number of things."

"What's that supposed to mean?"

I opened my eyes and once again faced him. "You're always in a panic when you don't know where I am."

"Don't you understand why?!" He was back to shouting.

"Of course I do!" Now I was shouting as well, all the while staring straight into his gorgeous eyes. There was no warmth in them though and his stares were icy. "If you think I don't relive that night every time I leave the house, you are highly mistaken! But I can't just stop living until I'm over the kidnapping and I discovered this weekend that I can't run away from it either."

I was rattled at this point but kept shouting as I spoke, not giving him a chance to comment. I did not want to hear anything he had to say at that moment.

"Just like I can't run from the memory of being trapped in a burning building, looking down the barrel of a gun pointed at me, being nearly beaten to death with a wine bottle, or your father's murder. I'm doing the best I can. So, what is it that you want from me?!" I slouched into the seat, breathing hard and breaking the staring contest we seemed to be having. I fought my hands' need to shake and clasped them together in order to keep them from doing so.

There was a long pause before he responded. His voice was no more than a whisper. "Why haven't you said that before? You never talk to me about that night. You never talk about any of the things that have happened to you since moving to Virginia. I just assumed you were managing it well."

'That night,' as we referred to it, was the night I was drugged and abducted by my late husband. So much happened in the couple of days that followed that night, I truly should not have survived it. Initially, I had no memory of the events that unfolded. As time passed, my memories began to return in fractured pieces, but my husband did not know that either.

"What did you think this trip was about? I am trying to deal with it all, but you keep bailing on me. Should I have gotten on the flight without you? I don't know. Should I have shut my phone off? Probably not. All I really knew was I needed to get away from here and I couldn't wait any longer."

I listened for Edward's response as exhaustion from the conversation made me close my eyes once again in an effort to try to relax. I was certain we were going to have this discussion for the entire hour trip to Thomas Hall and I was wishing I had not texted him announcing my impending arrival.

"Look at me," Edward said softly. When he had to repeat himself, his tone became edgier. "Look. At. Me."

I opened my eyes and Edward stared at me for what seemed like an eternity. He tilted his head side to side as though he were an artist, taking a close look at his newest subject.

"What?" I finally asked. Not able to understand his actions.

"What's happening to us? We weren't like this five months ago when we got married. We're both walking on eggshells. And when did we stop talking about the things that bother us?"

"When you stopped coming home." I sighed and when I looked at him, confusion was painted across his face. "What? Did you think the moment we came back from the honeymoon that working on this relationship was done and complete? That's not the way marriage works. I learned that the hard way."

He said nothing. I was not sure if it was because he was in denial that our relationship was imploding or if he just did not know what to say so I tried to help by prompting him. "What's bothering you?"

"My wife disappeared for three days with no one knowing where she was."

"Hold up for just a minute!" I snapped. His attitude about this trip was testing my last nerve. "I didn't disappear and you knew where to find me. You picked the hotel, remember? It wasn't my first choice. All you had to do was call the hotel or, better yet, catch the next flight. Don't accuse me of disappearing when you're the one who's always abandoning me." My voice started at a normal level but by the end it was shrill.

"Abandoning?" Edward repeated in the form of a question.

I shocked myself with the word choice, but it was the perfect word to describe how I felt.

"Yes. Abandoning." I swallowed hard as I finished my soda and looked out the window. Much to my surprise, we didn't speak for the rest of the trip home.

We had been home for several hours when, like in the car, I could no longer stand the silence. Despite the comfortable home I created, the tension in the air was suffocating from the moment we walked into it. I walked toward the door, slid on the sandals I wore home on the plane, grabbed my phone off the table by the entrance, and turned to Edward. He was sitting on the sofa staring at his laptop.

"I'm going for a walk." It was the first thing anyone had said since we arrived back at Thomas Hall.

He looked up from his computer and took his reading glasses off. He was even sexy wearing them. If I had not been angry with him, I would have dragged him off to bed right then. However, I was angry and he was once again displaying the stone-faced, emotionless expression he showed at the airport. "What do you want to do about dinner?"

"Whatever you want to do is fine. I won't be long."

I walked away from our house and instinctively headed toward the main house. I didn't go in even though the afternoon sun was beating down on me and the humidity left me feeling as though I had just stepped into a sauna. I continued to the willow tree. It had been the place of many picnics and even more kisses with Edward. I sat in the shade, leaning my back against its gigantic trunk, pulling my knees up to my chest, and wrapping my arms around them.

This was when I needed Sarah. Sarah Abbott was my best friend and roommate in college. She was more like a sister than a friend. She would have given me the most brutally honest advice. That's exactly what I needed now too. I went so far as to open my phone before I stopped myself. The Sarah I needed to talk to no longer existed. At the end of last year, many painful truths had come to light, testing our friendship, or at least what I thought our friendship had been. Inevitably though, our bond was severed beyond repair.

As I sat, I thought about how little of my life existed outside of Thomas Hall and felt the world close in on me. The weight of everything Edward and I talked about on the way home from the airport pressed against my chest. The pain was acute and I wrapped my arms tighter around my knees as my chest heaved up and down rapidly and tears slowly rolled down my face. I knew this was the start of another panic attack. I had never experienced one while Edward was at Thomas Hall with me and desperately tried to calm myself and I push the feelings down. I did not want him to stumble across me in this state.

Vivian, however, saw me through a window, made her way outside, and was walking towards the tree. She was a petite, thin woman. Always impeccably dressed as well as graceful, even when under duress. As she approached, I mumbled under my breath, "Not now. Not now."

I was fairly certain she had noticed the panic attacks before but had been kind enough not to say anything to me about it. When she reached me, she sat next to me on the mossy ground.

"You're back. How was Bermuda?" She asked, politely ignoring the visible signs of my panic attack and trying to distract me. "Please tell me you enjoyed yourself."

"Honestly, it was terrible. I love Bermuda, I always have, but it wasn't the trip I needed it to be. I guess my expectations were too high." She put her arms around me and I rested my head against her shoulder.

"Maybe they were, but I knew you wouldn't stay gone long. I told Edward if he was that worried about you to get on a plane and go to Bermuda."

I lifted my head off her and slightly nodded, unsure of what to say next.

"You aren't speaking to each other, are you?"

I shook my head.

"Not at all?"

"We spoke *at* each other in the car on the way home from the airport. I'm not certain it was in any way *to* each other." I closed my eyes and let my head fall forward until my chin was resting on my knees.

She gently rubbed my back as she spoke. "What's going on? Regardless of what you previously told me; something is very wrong. It's obvious you are not happy. And when you're not happy, Edward's not happy."

"I can't be responsible for his happiness, Vivian."

"That's not really fair though, is it? You expect him to be responsible for yours."

I opened my eyes, lifted my head, and looked at her. "I don't think that's true. But I do expect him to keep his promises."

"And he doesn't?"

I had to look away from her before I answered so I turned my attention towards the field of vines just past the house. The truth was far too painful. "He used to."

I waited for any questions or comments Vivian might make. She usually made me look at both sides of things when Edward and I argued. She was always the voice of reason. Instead, she sat with me, silently keeping me company. We sat for what seemed like a very long time but it was probably only about ten minutes. Then Vivian stood, brushed the grass and dirt from her slacks, and put out her hand to help me up. "Go home and talk it out. There is no other way around this."

I reluctantly walked down the path that led to our house, the sun now beating on the back of my neck. Vivian was right. There was nothing to do but talk this out. However, when I arrived home, the house was empty. No note, no evidence of where he had gone. I picked up my phone and dialed. Edward's phone went straight to voicemail. This was him exacting retribution. Doing to me what had happened to him. I had never known him to be this petty. His actions were pointless though because I wasn't worried about him. He was a big boy who could take care of himself.

I walked into the kitchen and opened the refrigerator. Thanks to the kitchen at Vivian's house, I had what I referred to as a magic refrigerator. I would leave for work and it would be empty, but by the time I would get home, there would be a few meals, snacks, fruit, and drinks. Occasionally there would be dessert as well. There was some chicken salad that wasn't there when I left Friday morning. I toasted a couple of pieces of bread and made myself a sandwich. I poured myself a glass of wine and watched tv in the living room while I ate. I was certain he would show up before the evening was out.

After dinner, I changed into a sky blue satin camisole and matching sleep shorts. I stretched out in our comfortable bed and read the latest viticulture journals. Our bedroom looked like something out of an Italian fairy tale. White shutters allowed privacy from the dark night and the drapes over the patio doors blocked out any view into our bedroom. The fresh flowers in the vase on the fireplace mantle, not provided by my husband but the cleaning staff, were cut from the gardens and greenhouse on the property. As I read, a wave of nausea swept over me. I wondered if the chicken salad was as fresh as I thought. However, as quickly as it arrived, it disappeared.

It was after eleven when I heard the creak of the front door's hinges. I walked into the living room and looked up and down at my husband. He did not have to say a word. His glassy eyes and relaxed body told me all I needed to know. Edward was drunk. Not so drunk he couldn't walk or speak clearly, but enough not to get behind the wheel of a car. While I knew he had not been driving as I heard no car engine as he arrived at the house. Exactly where and with whom he had gotten into this condition, I did not know. Nor did I care.

"Welcome home. Did you enjoy yourself?"

"No, not really."

"That's too bad. From the looks of the shape you're in, you are going to hate yourself in the morning. I'm going to bed." I turned to head back to the bedroom but before I took a single step, Edward gently and carefully placed his hand on my shoulder to stop me.

"Where do I get to sleep tonight?" There was no anger or frustration in his voice, just an honest question. It was the closest thing to tenderness I heard from Edward since before leaving for Bermuda.

"Wherever you like," I replied. "I'm going to sleep in our bed. You can sleep in there with me, take the guest room, the sofa, or go up to the main house. It's really your call."

"So, you're not kicking me out of the house?" At that moment, I realized he had fully expected to find a locked door when he came home. I had once, in anger, thrown Edward out of our home when we were still engaged. It was at the end of a fight that started with him revealing a damning secret that could have completely changed the direction of my life. It ended with me kicking him out of his own home.

"I promised you I would never do that again. And unlike you, I keep my promises." I probably should have not said the last sentence aloud, but in my opinion, it made a necessary point. I wondered though if Edward would even remember this conversation in the morning.

I was about to turn off the bedside light when Edward came in from the bathroom, dressed for bed in black sleep pants and gray t-shirt. I waited for him to sit on the bed before I turned off the light. Once settled, he moved closer until he was spooned against me and rested his hand on my hip. If he had stopped there,

I would have let him stay in that position. He did not. Instead, he whispered in my ear, "Goodnight Cassie. I love you, Baby," and kissed my neck. I lifted his hand off my hip, placed it on the mattress, and slid my body away from him. He was so drunk he forgot that I hated being called baby.

"Goodnight, Edward."

Chapter Six

I WOKE THE NEXT morning just as the sun began to illuminate the night sky. Sunrise wouldn't happen for another hour. I was laying against Edward in our oversized bed, my head resting on his chest and one leg wrapped around his. He had his arms around me, holding me tight. This was not an unusual way for us to find each other first thing in the morning. However, on this particular morning, it was awkward and I was cold. The air conditioning had run most of the night and the air reminded me of a hospital, icy and sterile. I lifted the comforter with the intention of getting out of bed. Edward immediately pulled it back onto us and tightened his grip on me a little more.

"You're awake," he said.

"Yes."

"Did you get any sleep?"

"A little," I said as I tried to wiggle out of his arms.

"Please, don't pull away from me," he whispered with desperation in his voice and kept his arms snug around me. "Let's do this right here. Like this."

"Do what?"

"Talk this out."

"What is there to say?"

"A lot, I think. Yesterday's discussion in the car gave me a lot to think about."

"You start then," I said.

Edward placed my hand, which was laid across his chest, in his and we both watched as he played with my fingers intertwining with his. "Abandoned. Are you really feeling that way?"

It took less than a second to consider the word once again. There was no hesitation in my response. "Yes."

"Okay. When? How?"

"I'm not sure I understand what you're asking for, Edward."

"You're avoiding the question." I put my chin on his chest and looked up at him as irritation crept in. But he was hungover. The kind of hangover that takes a couple of days to get out of your system so I let the attitude slide.

"No, I'm not. When? When what? When did I start feeling like this? When did I first realize something was wrong? When did it get unbearable? When could be a lot of different things." I successfully untangled myself from him as I spoke. "Stay put, I'll be right back."

I stood up, went into the kitchen, and returned with two bottles of water and a bottle of Tylenol. I handed a bottle of water to Edward, opened the medicine, and fished two pills out for him. I watched as he took the pills and downed the whole bottle of water.

I set the second bottle on the bedside table and crawled back into bed, placing myself as near as possible to my previous position.

"Maybe how is the better place to start," I said, laying my head back on his chest and making my hand available for him to hold.

"Okay, how did this happen?" He asked, his voice soft and caring.

I sighed. "I know that no matter how I try to say this, it's going to start another argument."

"If it needs to be said, say it."

"Okay. How? How you seem to forget that your wife should be a priority." I mentally braced myself for a quick, defensive response. I was surprised by his calm reply.

"Tell me exactly what part of that I've forgotten, Sweetie."

"I want you. Not flowers, not expensive jewelry, and especially not excuses for *not* coming home on a weeknight." In the last two months, I received flowers from him on five different occasions along with three blue boxes from Tiffany's with various pieces of jewelry. It was all extravagant, but the only thing I wanted was the one thing I was not getting, Edward's time.

"Now we're getting somewhere."

"What do you mean?" I tilted my head to get a better look at his unshaven face.

"Sweetie, you knew what you were getting into when we got married. I work. It's what I do. I have a company to run. People depend on me."

"Yes, but I feel like you promised me a life you're not delivering on. When we got married you were at Thomas Hall four nights a week. Sometimes more. Now you show up on Saturday mornings and leave on Sundays after lunch with a promise of Wednesday night." I dropped my voice to a whisper. "Only to cancel Wednesday afternoon. It's not what I signed up for. I'm sorry, it's just not enough."

"You could come to D.C."

"I do. And spend the whole time in that god-awful town, sitting in your god-awful apartment alone while you work." I could feel the tears welling up in my eyes. I squeezed my eyelids shut to keep them from rolling down my face.

"I told you if you don't like the apartment, then redecorate it."

"It's not about the apartment, Edward!" I had not intended on screaming but my frustration left me no choice. I took a deep breath and lowered my voice before continuing. "It's about us. There is no us. There's Edward. There's Cassandra. But not us. Not anymore."

"That's not true."

"Then tell me," I said as I locked eyes with him. "What was the last thing we did as a couple besides sleep in the same bed one night a week and have Sunday lunch with your mother?"

He opened his mouth to speak, but nothing came out. He was thinking hard about it. I knew it would take a while for him to think of something because I could not even remember anything myself. Seconds turned into minutes. I slid myself up along his body until we were eye to eye and my head was propped up on my hand next to him. He slowly looked over my body, admiring it, before his soft lips brushed against mine and then leaned in for a regretful kiss. "Good God Cassie, why didn't you say something sooner?"

"That's my fault. I should have said something long before now."

"I wish you had. It was so gradual that I didn't even see what I was doing. But I can fix this. It might take a little time to clear my schedule, but I can change this."

At first, I hoped he decided to let the Bermuda trip go with no further discussion but knew I wasn't going to get off that easily. Upon reflection though, I realized I had more to say than he probably did. So, I didn't wait for him. I put my chin on his shoulder and rested my head on his pillow.

"I guess we need to talk about Bermuda, huh?"

"Probably should. You said you had to get on that plane. Why?"

"I'm not sure where to begin," I said, truly at a loss of where to start.

"Start wherever you want. It doesn't matter. Just talk to me, Sweetie. I want to understand."

I took a moment and a deep breath in an attempt to center my thoughts before I began. "I know it appears that I travel just for the sake of adventure and I let people believe that. But that's not completely true."

"Really?" Edward's expression, which I usually read well, was that of genuine shock.

"You never noticed that once I arrived at Thomas Hall, I stopped traveling? It was because I was content with my life. I travel when I'm distressed or need to figure things out."

"You run away to escape your problems."

"Not so much run away, I think," I said hesitantly. "I just put some space between me and the problem so I can gain perspective."

"You do realize that is the very definition of running away?"

I continued speaking, not acknowledging his question. "I really believed if we could get away, we could fix what was going on with us. But you kept bailing. And when you texted, bailing on the trip yet again, I realized I was going to have to figure it out by myself."

He turned his body to face me and wrapped his arms around me. We were so close to one another that our foreheads touched.

"Cassie," he whispered. "How the hell am I supposed to know that? I'm not a mind reader. Should I have realized things were going off the rails sooner? Yes. But I can't know what you don't tell me."

"I know. I'm sorry. I need to work on that too. For so many years I couldn't speak my mind without terrible consequences. Now that I can, it often doesn't even occur to me to say anything." My first marriage had been strained at best and violent on a regular basis. This unfortunate baggage seemed to constantly control the life Edward and I were trying to build together. I was aware of its impact and was trying to change, but old habits die hard.

He tilted his head until our lips found each other. As his kisses moved from my lips to my neck, I began to think that things were going to get better.

"This can all be fixed. You need to promise me something though. From now on you've got to tell me when things are going wrong and not wait until they are so bad that this happens again. Do you understand? I love you. I don't ever want to see you as unhappy as you've been for the last couple of months."

I nodded my head and I found his warm, soft lips pressed against mine again.

"Cassie, in light of what you just told me, I want to ask you something. But I don't want you to think I'm still mad at you." He paused and I nodded my head, confirming that I understood. "Do you think it's possible that you subconsciously left your phone off to put some distance between you and your problem, being me, so you could think things through?"

I rolled onto my back, still in Edward's arms, and stared at the ceiling. The room was becoming brighter as the sun was now creeping above the horizon. I wondered if I could have done such a thing and not even been aware of it. "I don't know. Maybe? Regardless, I really am sorry about that. You must have been a wreck."

He sighed and ran his fingers through his hair before pulling me even closer to him.

"You have no idea. Promise me, if you ever feel the need to run away from home again that you will leave your cell phone on."

"Okay. I will, but I doubt I'll ever do something like that again. It was such a lonely trip without you."

Silence filled the room. Then, after a few minutes, I heard a quiet snore. It was barely audible at first but grew in volume over a five-minute span. There were very few occasions Edward snored, but I should have seen it coming. He was hungover and my guess was he had not slept well the last couple of nights.

Chapter Seven

I SAT IN THE living room reading a book on the history of alchemy and finished my first cup of hot tea. I had nothing on my schedule for the day as we were supposed to be in Bermuda until late in the evening. I heard Edward's phone ring in the bedroom until it went to voicemail. Moments later, my phone rang. It was Edward's assistant, Kelly.

"Good morning, Kelly," I began when I answered the phone.

"Good morning. Do you know what time Edward left Thomas Hall? He's not at the apartment so I'm guessing he was there last night. His nine o'clock appointment is here and he's not."

I blew out a deep breath and counted silently to ten before I intended to answer. However, what came out of my mouth was a question. "When did this go on Edward's schedule?"

"About two weeks ago. He scheduled it himself. Why?"

This was not the first time Edward had deceived me, so I should have known it would happen again. The other times he had done so in an effort to "protect me" but this was different. This did not protect me. It hurt me. It was a deception on top of a lie. It took every bit of strength I had to answer Kelly's question.

"Well, Edward is still here at Thomas Hall. Hungover and asleep."

"Did you say hungover?" She whispered.

"You should probably clear the day."

"The whole day? Cassandra, he's got back-to-back meetings until six tonight."

"I'd start clearing the morning then. I'll go wake him in a few minutes and have him call you back about the remainder of the day." My jaw muscles were tight and my lips pressed together.

He had never intended on going away. Not with appointments on his schedule made two weeks earlier. I felt my entire body tense. This hurt more than anything my abusive first husband had done to me. The fact remained, I was married to Edward now and I had to do everything possible to make our marriage work, regardless of my sudden feeling that it was a lost cause.

"While I've got you on the phone, I need you to add something to Edward's schedule."

"Sure, let me get his calendar pulled up." I could hear the clicking of her laptop keys. "Okay, what date?"

"Wednesday."

"Which Wednesday?"

"All of them. Put nothing on them after four in the afternoon. As a matter of fact, do the same for Fridays."

Kelly paused before she asked her next question. "For how long?"

"Indefinitely."

"That may be difficult. Probably impossible."

"The logistics of his schedule is not my job. Figure it out please." My anger seeped through each word.

There was a long silence before Kelly responded. "Cassandra, what's going on? I can tell something is not right."

I blew out a deep breath before I answered. "I'm sorry, Kelly. That was rude of me. Edward and I were supposed to be in Bermuda today. So, the fact that Edward put something on his calendar two weeks ago, tells me he had no intention of making our Friday morning flight."

"What flight?" A slight panic crept into her voice. "He never mentioned needing to catch a flight."

"I'm not surprised."

"I swear to God, he told me nothing about Bermuda."

"I believe you. Please just try to make my scheduling request work. The future of my marriage may very well depend on it."

After we said our goodbyes, I walked into our bedroom, yanked the heavy chocolate-colored raw silk drapes covering a sliding glass door open, and allowed the day's bright sun to pour over the bed. Edward woke immediately, groaning as he squinted.

"What the hell, Cassie?"

"What. The. Hell." I said quietly. I was so angry I could not even scream at him, but tears rolled down my face. "Kelly just called. Your nine o'clock meeting, the one you scheduled two weeks ago, is waiting for you to arrive at your office in D.C. You never intended on making the flight Friday, did you?"

"Kelly must have accidentally put—"

"Don't try to put this on her. She didn't even know we had rescheduled the trip. I can't believe you would not only do this, but you would wait until I was at the gate for the flight before you said anything."

Edward was now sitting on the edge of the bed. He reached up to touch my arm, but I pulled away.

"Don't." I was certain the disappointment and heartbreak were written all over my face and I had no intention of trying to mask it. "You should probably call Kelly back. She needs to know what to do with the rest of your day." I wrapped my arms around my torso, hugging myself, and walked out of the room.

I was debating on what to do next when my phone rang again. This time it was Alex. I answered and put it on speakerphone, walking into the kitchen to make another cup of ginger peach tea.

"I know you are technically still on vacation, but I finally got news about the dead vines and thought you'd want to know." His voice sounded hoarse and quiet.

"You sound worse than Edward this morning. What in the world did y'all drink last night?" If two of the three brothers were hungover, it was a safe assumption that all three spent the evening drinking and commiserating about their love lives. My guess was Henry, Edward's middle brother, was in the worst shape of all even though his relationship was probably the most stable of the three brothers. He could not hold his liquor as well as his siblings.

"Bourbon, Tequila, Beer," Alex replied. "And way too much of all of it. I don't think I'll ever drink again."

I laughed. "Serves you right. Do you want to tell me about the vines over the phone or should I walk down to the office?" As I asked the question, I heard the shower turn on in the bathroom.

"I may as well do it now. They were poisoned. Someone injected a glyphosate solution into them. The lab noticed the drilled holes in the *pied de vigne*."

"The foot of the vine?" I was surprised at how often I used my French language knowledge at Thomas Hall.

"Yes, I missed it because I wasn't thinking poison. Whoever did this poured the same solution around them as well. We tested the soil too. This clean-up is going to be a monster."

"Why would someone use weed killer on the vines?"

"I don't know who or why," he said, with an edge to his voice, "but someone is trying to kill my baby." The winery truly was Alex's baby. He loved and cared for it as if he had birthed it himself.

"Alex, are you familiar with the ransom of Romanée-Conti in Bordeaux in 2010? Something similar to this happened there."

"Yeah, I would say I'm surprised that you're familiar with that incident, but your brain is an endless well of knowledge. That incident came with ransom notes, complete with demands, directions, and maps. To the best of my knowledge, we've received no such thing."

"Same here," I said. "Can you check and see if anyone at the production building received anything?"

"Of course."

"I guess this means I need to call Brian and file a police report. He's got to be sick of doing paperwork with my name on it. Thank God we're friends."

Brian Hayes was a police detective for the town of Willow Creek and one of my dearest friends. He was my window into the real world which was often a far cry from the fairytale existence I had been pulled into when I met my husband. In addition, he was a single father to twin girls, who were about to become teenagers.

His lagoon blue eyes were his most prominent feature and he was tall, with broad shoulders, and muscular arms. His salt and pepper hair was cut military short when we first met, but his girls convinced him to let it grow out. Brian's girls were right. His longer hair made him look younger, even though it still never touched the collar of his shirt.

As soon as we wrapped up the call, I dialed Brian's number. I needed to talk to him about something else too. I had yet to apologize for not returning his texts while I was in Bermuda. He answered the phone in true Brian form.

"Hey, the gypsy returns!"

"Yeah, about that. I'm sorry I didn't answer your texts. I turned my phone off for the outbound flight and forgot to turn it back on."

"That sounds like you," Brian said.

"At least someone believes me."

"Cassandra, what's happened between you and Edward? Between him calling me begging for me to text you while you were away and what you just said, I'm pretty sure there's trouble in paradise."

"It's nothing, really. Just some miscommunications." My relationship with Edward was the one thing I would not talk about with Brian. Early in our friendship Brian made it clear he was open to being more than just friends. As tempting as the offer was, I was not in love with him, so I declined.

There was something more though. My best friend and my husband had a past. One I could not get either to speak about.

A past that often gnawed at me. A past I never knew if I would find out about. So, I moved on from that thought and changed the subject. "Unfortunately, I'm calling in an official capacity."

Brian said the only thing I could imagine him saying. "Oh crap. Who's dead now?"

"Grapevines."

"Huh?"

I went on to explain to him everything that happened with the vines and what we'd discovered. After a little thought and discussion, Brian decided to meet with Alex and file the report with his statement since he would need to consult with him on getting copies of the lab results.

As we wrapped up the call, Edward came into the living room where I was sitting. He was wearing khaki pants and a light blue polo shirt, still barefoot, and towel drying his hair. I could not even look him in the eye. I knew if I did my heartbroken tears would begin to fall again and I was done with that.

"What time do you have to be at the office?" I asked.

"I'm not going in. I'm guessing you are going to want to talk about this some more."

I sat silently, contemplating how the last few hours had played out before saying anything at all. "No, I think we both said everything we needed to say earlier this morning. The last half hour is just more evidence that I'm no longer a priority. And if that didn't prove it, your lying to me did."

"Cassandra, I know I shouldn't have lied to you. I'm sorry, but—"

"No but," I said flatly. "If you have to add that then you aren't really sorry."

Chapter Eight

THE NEXT MORNING, I made myself a cup of hot tea and sat on the sofa in my office that overlooked a stunning view of the vines through the large window that ran ceiling to floor, watching it rain. I never found the sound calming, as the most tragic moments of my life had been punctuated by rain, thunder, and lightning. This morning the rain was no different and provided no comfort. Thoughts about my marriage filled my mind the moment Edward left for work and were now overflowing, not allowing for other concerns or emotions.

How much longer could I go on like this? I loved that man so much, but every time I heard or saw the words, *I'm sorry Sweetie, but...*, my heart shattered into more pieces. If I didn't love him, I probably wouldn't care and it probably wouldn't hurt. I only knew one person who had ever been this devastated by their spouse. I walked over to my desk and picked up the phone.

"Michael Abbott." He was the ex-husband of my former best friend, Sarah, as well as the best friend of my first husband.

He was not my type, but decent looking, and I understood Sarah's attraction to him when they first met. He had grown more handsome over the years, but Sarah was not satisfied with married life. Two years before they divorced, Michael had been crushed when he discovered his wife was having an affair with a co-worker in the office where both Michael and Sarah worked. They separated and reconciled only to later dissolve the marriage. When they decided to end their marriage, Sarah left the accounting firm Michael's father owned and Michael took over the accounting for Thomas Hall.

"Hi."

"Cassandra? What's wrong? Your voice sounds off." We had known each other for over a decade and he could tell a lot about me by the sound of my voice. It took me years to discover it, but Michael was incredibly sensitive to noticing when the people he cared about were not happy.

"Would you have any time this week when we could have lunch?" I heard my own voice cracking as I asked.

"Always. We could do it tomorrow if you like. But what is going on? I have a feeling this shouldn't wait."

"It's...it's my marriage. I'm thinking I might have made a big mistake." Despite my efforts, a tear rolled down my face.

"Keep talking." I heard papers being shuffled about on his desk at the accounting firm he was being groomed to take over from his father. "Tell me everything."

The whole story spilled out in a string of fractured thoughts. Edward's lack of coming home during the week. Making decisions about canceling trips without telling me, and how desperately lonely I had become. As I spoke, I realized that this, minus the physical and verbal abuse, sounded like a repeat of my first marriage and I rambled on about that as well. I have no idea how he understood anything, but Michael asked very few questions. When he did, it was only for clarification. He had known me long enough to understand the way my mind worked. I talked for what seemed like forever, which I would discover was just over an hour. Because as I finished, there was a knock on my office door. When I opened it, Michael was standing on the other side.

I stood in the doorway, my phone still in my hand. "Why didn't you tell me you were on the way?"

"I needed to see you. Make absolutely certain that you were physically fine." Michael had only found out about six months ago that my first husband had been physically abusive. He had yet to forgive himself for not seeing it when it was happening and needed confirmation that this was not happening again. "And we're having lunch today."

He embraced me in a long hug. This was exactly what I needed. A friend, one who would not talk to anyone in the family about what was said and would give me honest advice.

I made Michael a cup of coffee and a fresh cup of tea for me. We sat in silence on the sofa in front of the window. When he finished his coffee, he turned to me and asked, "How long has this been goin' on?" His Southern accent always seemed more pronounced out of the office.

"A couple of months. It was so gradual. I didn't see it at first. Then I found myself alone, almost all the time. As much as I hate D.C., I even considered moving there for a while. But even when I'm there, he's working and I'm alone someplace I don't want to be. At least I like being here."

"Have you talked with him about this?"

"Talked, cried, yelled, whispered. We've done it all. He says he's going to fix it, but..."

"But you don't believe him, do ya?"

"I want to. But I feel like I'm trying to teach an old dog new tricks. Maybe he's just too set in his ways. I guess this is what happens when you marry someone you've only known for two months. Why didn't you stop me?"

"I was going to say that's what happens when you marry someone over twenty years older than you."

I released a small growl from my throat. The age gap between Edward and I was a touchy subject for me of late. It did not bother me until after we married and I started attending corporate events with him. The looks and the whispers when we walked into a room were unnerving. Edward claimed it was jealousy. He was certain the men in the room wished they had a young, beautiful woman accompanying them. However, I knew the truth. It was not the men whispering, it was the women. I had a good idea of some of the things that were being said about me. Obviously, these people did not know me. Those who did knew I was neither a call girl nor a gold-digging slut. I knew it should not matter what other people thought, but I worried how their attitude concerning Edward and me could hurt his reputation within the business world.

"I know that people thought that it was a good enough reason for us not to marry."

"But do you really think anything or anyone could have stopped the two of ya? Especially after everything Tony put y'all through."

My late husband, Tony, who unbeknownst to me, had faked his own death. He reappeared mere weeks before Edward's and my wedding date. He wreaked havoc on our lives and the psychological fallout from Tony's reign of terror made both of us more determined to marry immediately.

"You're right. We were hellbent on making it to the altar," I said, followed by a long sigh. "Michael, what in the world was I thinking?"

"I have no idea, but I'm thinkin' I'm hungry. Let's go get an early lunch and talk about this some more."

Chapter Nine

IT WAS UNUSUAL FOR all of the Bakers to be in one room at the same time. However, on Sunday, all the adults were sitting at the dinner table for a family meal. And that meant family only. It was one of the few rules at Thomas Hall. Any other day, everyone was welcome at Vivian's table but on Sundays, if your last name wasn't Baker or White, you were not eating in the dining room. Alex was a Baker by blood but his mother, Senior's mistress, gave him her last name, White.

Poppy was in town, and no one would have said a word otherwise if he had joined us. However, Sunday night had become boys' night for Poppy and Victor. Victor ran the Thomas Hall Estate for years before retiring in January. He was a short, thin man with gray hair and a Yorkshire accent even though he had been in Virginia for over thirty years. He still lived on the grounds and the two men enjoyed talking with each other about their lives. Every Sunday the two went out for dinner at the Italian restaurant in town and regaled tales from their youth.

Phoebe's children were at their dad's house. Phoebe was Edward's only sister who currently resided in Richmond but thought nothing of making the hour drive whenever the mood struck her.

While I sat next to Edward, we did not engage in conversation. Even after a week, things were still tense between us. I found myself clenching my jaw, causing the muscles in my mouth to ache. My stomach, which had been churning for days, destroyed any desire for food. Henry was sitting on the other side of him, and they were in a deep discussion of the pros and cons of microbreweries and what it would take to get one up and running. Watching the two as they spoke, I was reminded that Henry was a carbon copy of his late father. He had the same blue eyes and broad-shouldered build. They were of similar height, about five foot eight and when Henry smiled, I saw Senior. Not only in his looks, but in his mannerisms, laugh, and facial expressions. I had a feeling I was about to lose my beloved brother-in-law to his own microbrewery. There was potential for it to be very successful. I had no idea who could replace him as the production supervisor if he left. One more thing for me to worry about.

Alex and Vivian were having a lighthearted conversation, which was very unusual as their personalities often clashed, when Phoebe, who seemed to be unaware of the events that transpired surrounding my recent trip, looked over and asked a question that brought all other conversations to a halt.

"Cassandra, did you and Edward have a good time in Bermuda?"

Suddenly, the silence was so palpable in the room that I found it necessary to pause before I spoke. I could feel Edward's eyes locked on my face but did not look at him. I swirled my spoon in the bowl of soup, debating on whether to eat it as I responded. Usually, I would have devoured the clam chowder, but the fresh reminder of the week's events left me with a sour taste in my mouth after only one spoonful.

"Edward bailed on the trip, again." I had thrown Edward to the sharks, but at that moment I still had no sympathy for him.

Vivian was quick to ask the next question. "What do you mean *again*?"

"It was the third time we scheduled the trip. So, I went alone."

Vivian looked over at Phoebe. "Can you believe your brother?"

Phoebe stared at Henry. "Is our brother really that stupid?"

"Hey, I'm sitting right here," Edward cut in.

"So you are," Henry commented and that's when he smacked his brother in the back of the head.

It was then I understood why the whole family was there. This was an intervention. The question about Bermuda was orchestrated to start the conversation. The family was trying to keep me from leaving Edward by giving him what my father would have called a "Come to Jesus" moment. Basically, a wake-up call to make him understand the consequences of his recent behavior.

I snorted out a muffled laugh, stood up, and walked out of the room. I did not need to be present for the remainder of this discussion. I was barely out the dining room door and into the hall when I heard the normally soft voice of Henry bellow across the room and into the rest of the first floor. Curiosity got the better of me so I stopped and listened.

"You idiot! You didn't tell me it was the third time you blew off the trip."

"Why should it make a difference?"

"Because," Henry said, raising the volume of his voice even more, "you are one more stupid decision away from her leaving you!"

"She won't divorce me," Edward replied confidently. "She has said it a hundred times, she doesn't believe in divorce. You saw what it did to her when she thought she would have to divorce Tony."

"She won't divorce you brother, but there isn't much doubt she could, and would, leave you," Phoebe interjected.

"Edward, she's not the same girl that showed up here in September." I did not think Alex would elaborate, but he continued. "She's changed. You've been a big part of that change too. Cassandra is more confident about her decisions, determined enough to not fear following through on what she desires, and willing to act in the name of self-preservation if she's unhappy. And whether you realize it or not, she's sacrificed a lot to make this relationship work."

"Like what?" Edward earnestly asked Alex, who had so succinctly summed up the last eight months of my life.

"If you'd been here, you would know now, wouldn't you?" Phoebe confidently questioned her brother, knowing full and well he was screwing up his marriage.

"The napkin throwing was uncalled for, don't ya think?" Edward asked. I could envision Phoebe balling up her dinner napkin and throwing it at her brother's face. I smiled.

"She's struggling too," Vivian said, not wanting her children's antics to distract from the purpose of the conversation. The smile left my face. I was not thrilled she noticed. I guess I was not as good at hiding it as I thought. "I'm assuming you know about the panic attacks."

"What panic attacks?" Edward asked, concern lacing his words.

"She tries to hide them, but they're getting worse. She battled one while we were having lunch with my sisters at the country club the day before she left for Bermuda. She thought no one noticed, but everyone at our table did."

"She had one a couple of weeks ago when we were shopping," Phoebe added. "I thought she was going to pass out. She claimed her blood sugar was dropping, but I didn't buy it."

"Why have I never seen one?" Edward asked.

"She only has them when the two of you are apart. The more you aren't here, the more frequently they happen." Vivian paused for a brief moment before continuing. "Are you starting to understand what you need to do or should I spell it out for you, Son?"

There was no reply. The silence was like an invisible fog that suffocated everyone in the house. I knew dessert would be served in the sitting room, so I made my way there to see what would happen next, even though I had no desire to eat.

What followed was unexpected. Edward walked into the sitting room, closed and locked the door, and then unceremoniously dropped himself at the other end of the sofa. I closed the magazine I was skimming through and looked at him. He had run his fingers through his hair one too many times and his normally perfect hair was now a tousled mess.

"Were you planning on telling me about these panic attacks?" He did not sound angry but his voice was not gentle either.

"No, I wasn't."

"Why not?" His voice sounded gruff and I knew his patience was waning.

I shrugged my shoulders and he slid down the sofa, closer to me, obviously concerned. He reached over a took my hand. "How long have you been having them, Sweetie?"

"Since we got back from our honeymoon."

"That was six months ago. Why haven't you said anything?" He sounded hurt that I withheld this part of my life from him.

"At first, I thought they might go away in time. When I realized that wasn't going to happen, you were never around to talk about it. I mean, I wasn't going to waste our one night a week together hashing out something I didn't want to talk about to begin with. When was I supposed to tell you? When you texted me to tell me you're not coming home?" I sighed and then continued. "So, you text me with the standard *Sorry Sweetie, but I'm not going to make it home tonight.* And you really expect me to respond with *That's fine. Oh, and by the way, I had two panic attacks today. Have a nice night*?"

Edward sat in silence, staring at me. I knew he would have nothing to say. After a minute of reflection, he decided to move on to another topic. "I'm assuming you heard Henry."

"Everyone in a three-county radius heard Henry," I replied, allowing the corners of my mouth to turn upward.

"Is he right?"

"About?"

"Come on, Cassandra. You're going to make me repeat it?"

I looked into his beautiful brown eyes, possibly for the first time that day, forcing his attention. I saw fear and panic reflected back at me. The smirk left my face. I was going to make him say it. I needed to know, without a doubt, that Edward understood what was at stake.

"Is Henry right about what?"

"Me being one stupid decision away from losing you."

I needed him to hear it and I was not going to lie to him either. "I honestly can't tell you that I haven't considered leaving. Edward, if we never see each other, what's the point?"

Chapter Ten

Monday morning Edward woke me up with a kiss on my neck as he prepared to leave. I was surprised when he decided to stay at Thomas Hall Sunday night. "I'm off to D.C. See you tonight." I am fairly certain I mumbled a goodbye before rolling over and returning to a peaceful slumber.

It wasn't until I was completely awake a couple of hours later, walking to my office in the production building, that I remembered what he said. It had to be a mistake. Edward was never home on Monday nights. Not even when he came home four or five nights a week, he always stayed in D.C. on Monday nights. "Wouldn't that be nice though," I said to myself but shook the thought off.

A little after six that evening, I heard the front door open. I peeked around the corner from the kitchen where I was staring into the open refrigerator contemplating what to do about dinner. I watched as my husband sat his briefcase on the desk and draped his suit jacket over the chair next to it. I stepped into the doorway, and he saw me, no doubt looking shocked, as he made his way to where I stood.

"How was your day, Sweetie?" He asked as his strong arms engulfed me and pulled me close for a kiss. I took a long moment to enjoy his warm, tender lips pressed against mine.

"Don't misunderstand me. I'm always happy to see you, but what are you doing here on a Monday night?"

"Making some changes. Is this a problem?"

"No. Just surprising."

He pulled away to get a better look at my face. I managed a weak smile. I was truly happy to see him, but I knew how this would play out. For a week, maybe even two, he would play the devoted husband and come home as much as possible. Then it would taper off to two or three nights a week and before I knew it, I would be back to having Edward at home with me once a week.

"What's the dinner plan?" He asked.

"I don't have one. I didn't expect you home. I figured I'd have leftovers or make myself a peanut butter and jelly sandwich. I haven't had much of an appetite lately."

He smiled. "Well, those options hardly seem sufficient." He pulled out his cell phone and called the kitchen at the main house. Within the hour, we were sitting at the dinner table, completely set with linen tablecloths and lit candles. The kitchen staff had miraculously put together a beautiful three-course meal, complete with a spinach salad, eggplant parmesan, toasted Italian bread, and gelato for dessert.

After dinner, we sat in the living room, drinking the wine we opened with our meal. I was curled up at one end of the sofa and Edward was at the other, his feet propped up on the coffee table.

Normally, I would be snuggled up against him, practically sitting on his lap, but I still needed physical space. He had lied to me, and I wasn't completely over it yet.

"So, will Monday nights be a regular thing?"

"Yes, and so will every other night of the week as well."

"Edward, please don't make promises you won't keep."

"I'm not. I'm going to start coming home every night I possibly can."

Edward must have seen the reluctance I was trying to mask. I wanted to say something, but before I could form the words, Edward continued.

"I know you don't believe me and I get it. You have no reason to trust me right now, not after Bermuda, but I told you I am going to fix this." He paused for a moment and then shook his head. "No, not *this*. I'm going to fix *me*.

"My family did everything an intervention group should at dinner last night, minus actually shipping me off to rehab. I spent most of the day thinking about it. I got my ass kicked by my family, not just because they love me, but because they love you and are afraid they're going to lose you because I've been an idiot.

"I promise you, Sweetie, I'm going to make things right. I don't know why I've had my head stuck in the sand like an ostrich, but I'm paying attention now. And I won't ever stop."

I sighed deeply, praying he was right. "Time will tell, I suppose."

Tuesday morning was a repeat of Monday. His lips lightly pressed against my neck and a whisper woke me. "I'm off to work. I'll see you tonight."

I was prepared Tuesday evening when he walked in the door, even though I half expected him not to show. I called the kitchen at the main house earlier in the day, giving them more time to prepare. My cooking skills, which were non-existent when I first moved into our house were now minimal at best. There were four things I could make for a meal. Five if you included peanut butter and jelly sandwiches. The staff arrived around five thirty, set the table, and placed the prepared plates in the oven to keep the food warm.

Just as he had the previous evening, Edward arrived home just after six. I greeted him at the door with a kiss. "How are you doing this? The commute into and out of D.C. is horrible and using the helicopter daily isn't practical for a multitude of reasons. I'd be exhausted doing it two days in a row."

"I bought a new limo and hired a new driver. He isn't employed by Chesapeake Biotech or part of the family fleet. His sole objective is to commute me to and from work as quickly and efficiently as possible. Part of the reason I haven't been coming home as much is that by the end of the day, I've been too tired to deal with the traffic to get out of D.C. Now I can leave earlier and finish up work in the car or catch a nap if I'm tired."

I had been concerned about Edward's health for the last six months. Every time I leaned against him, his heart sounded like he was running a marathon. I wondered if the exhaustion was a symptom of something more than a busy day at work but quickly dismissed the thought.

"Oh, I see," I said slowly, stretching each word with a whispered voice. Maybe he was serious about coming home every night. I wanted to believe him, but that little voice in the back of my head warned me it was only temporary.

After dinner, we once again sat in the living room, drinking the wine opened earlier that evening just as we had the night before. I stared at my husband. I liked having him here every night. While I did not trust him of late to keep his promises, I missed being close to him. I had nearly forgotten it all. The sound of his voice, the way he brushed the back of his hand against my cheek, his beautiful smile. Just being in the same room with him made me happy.

I sat my now empty glass on the coffee table and slid down the sofa until I was snuggled up to him. "I could get used to this."

"Good, I already am. There is one thing though. I do have to fly to Atlanta Thursday night for a Friday morning meeting, but I'll be home in time for dinner Friday night."

I remembered him talking about this meeting. It had been scheduled for months. I knew he was not trying to avoid being at Thomas Hall, but this was probably the beginning of the end of him being home most nights. We weren't even through with week one and he was already skipping a night.

The strain in our relationship had me longing for the feelings we had when we first met. I knew one thing we could do that might help. It certainly could not hurt. So, I took his wine glass from him, put it on the table, and stood up all the while holding his hand. "Let's go to bed."

"Isn't it a little early to go to sleep? It's not even eight o'clock."

"Who said anything about sleep?" His lips formed into one of his Cheshire cat grins as he stood and we walked hand in hand across the room, moving in the direction of the bedroom.

Our sex life varied greatly, depending on our collective mood. Sometimes we were vocal and passionate, other times involved laughter and fun. On this occasion, there was total silence. Two bodies intertwined. No words. No laughter. Just quiet surrender. His eyes, lips, and hands gently connected with me until no parts of my body were left untouched. I had long memorized every inch of his body but found myself doing the same as well.

After, we lay spooning with only a sheet covering us, the weight of his left arm draped across my torso. Edward lowered his head until he could whisper in my ear and his lips grazed my skin as he spoke.

"Does this mean I'm out of the doghouse?"

"No," I said turning my body to face him and resting a hand along his cheek.

"Then I'm confused. Why are we in bed together?"

"Edward, I love you. I want to be with you. I just don't know if I can live the way we have these last few months." The words *I love you* coming from me always made an impact. I said them more often now than I ever had in my life. However, my own husband had maybe only heard the words from my mouth a handful of times over the course of our entire relationship.

Edward smiled, acknowledging my words of affection. He pulled me closer and kissed my temple. "I love you too. And I told you, I'm working on it."

"Time will tell, I suppose."

"You've been saying that a lot lately."

"What?" I asked.

"Time will tell. I've never heard you say that phrase until recently."

I closed my eyes and turned my body away from him so we could resume spooning before I replied. Spooned up against him was my happy place.

"It's a reminder to myself to be patient and in time things can change." I hesitated and clamped my mouth tight. Edward sensed it.

"You wanted to say something more. Something about time and change maybe?" He knew me well.

"Yeah, it's a thing about time. Do you remember when I was in the hospital?"

"Which time?"

I chuckled sarcastically even though it was not really all that amusing. "The time after Tony died."

"I remember." Just the thought upset him and his tone gave that away.

"Do you remember the doctor telling me I may or may not ever remember what happened to me during the kidnapping because of how Tony drugged me?"

"Yeah," he paused, and the sound of him sucking the oxygen from the room told me he knew what was about to be said.

It was as if my mouth was full of cotton. I tried to swallow the feeling down and speak, but no words came out. Edward quickly flipped me around in his arms so we were face to face. He found me biting my bottom lip.

"You remember then?"

"Bits and pieces." Things from that event flashed through my mind and you could hear my jagged breaths as I struggled to speak.

"It seems like there's a little more each time. I remember the phone call." As soon as I said it, I watched the color drain from Edward's face.

While Tony held me hostage, he called Edward demanding a ransom. He feared I was already dead and demanded to speak to me. Initially, I did not remember our conversation and Edward refused to tell me what I said. He knew it would upset me. And when I remembered, it was heart-shattering.

I climbed on top of Edward, straddled him, and burrowed my face into his neck. I hated the way everything I remembered made me feel. I just wanted it all to go away. There was nothing more to say or do except be in that moment of him holding me. And that's what he did. He silently held me in our bed and waited. He and I could both feel the buildup to my having a nervous breakdown. I had experienced them before and one landed me in a hospital. Eventually, I slid my body off of his but stayed tangled in his arms.

"Do you want to talk about it?"

"No. I don't think so and I don't think I ever will."

"Okay. Have you at least told your therapist?" Immediately after the kidnapping, Edward insisted on helping me find a therapist. I knew many people found it helpful to have a professional to talk with about their problems. I was not one of those people.

"I stopped seeing her about a month and a half ago. It was going nowhere and I was wasting both her time and mine."

"Why didn't you tell me you stopped seeing her?"

I sighed before I spoke. He didn't get it yet. "You weren't here to tell."

There was a long silence. I wished I could make him see how important his presence was to me.

"Sweetie, maybe you should look for a new therapist," he said, trying hard to encourage me to continue therapy but using a tone that did not sound pushy. "Sometimes it takes a couple before finding one that's a good fit and I think you need one more than you realize."

"I don't know. Maybe, but not right now." I felt the weight of these memories lift as soon as I told him I was beginning to remember that night. Regardless though, the discussion left me feeling especially vulnerable.

"Edward, are we going to be okay? I feel like we're losing each other. And I need you. I don't think I understood how much I need you until just now." My voice sounded small and timid.

Edward pressed my head into his chest, weaving his fingers into my hair and kissing the top of my head. "Of course, we will." He ran his fingers through my long, black hair, playing with the length of it as it slipped through his fingers. As he did, I heard him whisper, "Time will tell. I promise."

The nightmares about 'that night' were happening more and more and the ones that night were the worst so far. It centered around the phone conversation that happened while I was tied to a bed in a filthy motel room. Edward did the only thing he could do to help. He held me. The next morning found me sleep-deprived and exhausted from the restless night. So much so that I decided to work from home.

Chapter Eleven

I looked twice in my rear-view mirror as I passed through the winery gate, heading into town. Most days leaving the winery would have been a good thing and included lunch with friends or shopping, but today it was rushed, and my little Volkswagen Beetle was flying down country roads to get to town. A panicked call from the hospital put me into rescue mode. My best friend's twins called me from the nurses' station. They could not reach their father, Brian, and their babysitter had been rushed to the hospital. The girls called 911 after their babysitter collapsed in the kitchen. The paramedics, who knew their dad, took them to the hospital as well, rather than leave them at home alone.

It took me less than fifteen minutes to get to the hospital and make my way to the emergency room. It wasn't until I walked through the door that I realized I was still in black yoga pants, a green tank top, along with a long cardigan and tennis shoes. It had become my weekday at-home uniform, but it probably wasn't the best image for me as the head of Thomas Hall Winery.

Before I could give it another thought, Gina and Georgie both were pressed against me, their arms wrapped tightly around me. They were nearly thirteen years old but seemed tiny for their age. They both had struggled with health issues at birth, and I was certain it was a factor in their size. They were pretty girls though. Long, straight, dark hair framed their porcelain-skinned faces and their big brown eyes suited them.

"Are you both okay?" I asked. They nodded their heads but failed to loosen their grip.

We stood silently for a moment longer before Georgie spoke. "That was really scary."

"I'm sure it was."

"What do we do now?" Gina asked.

"Let me see what's going on with Mrs. Whitmore and then we'll come up with a plan." I pried the girls off me, pointed them in the direction of two chairs, and headed to the information desk.

I was nearly there when Brian tore through the doors of the emergency room with the speed and energy of a Tasmanian devil. He saw me and ran to where I stood, grabbing me by the shoulders.

"The twins. Where are they? What happened? God, please tell me that they're okay!"

"Brian breathe. The girls are fine. Turn around. They're right behind you."

He turned and saw the girls' faces and when he did, I saw his shoulders drop out of their tense state and his jaw loosen as the tension left his body. He made his way directly to them.

A doctor walked up to me. He was new. I knew this after spending too much time as a patient at Community General

Hospital since moving to Virginia less than a year ago. "Hi. I'm Dr. Seymore Holt. Are you the twins' mother?"

I chuckled and decided not to explain that I would have been a mother at age fourteen if I had given birth to them. "No, just a family friend."

"Oh. The resemblance between you and the girls is quite striking. Can you let their parents know that those two young ladies probably saved Mrs. Whitmore's life?" I had not noticed it before but the girls did look like me. Minus the eye color, the similarities were endless.

"You can tell their father yourself. He's right there with them."

The tall, thin doctor walked over to Brian. It was only then I realized I was in a large, crowded space. I could feel the panic building in me. So many people. I could disappear and no one would notice. When this feeling bubbled to the surface, so did the nauseousness and chills that came with it and it left me frozen in place.

"Cassandra, are you okay? You look terrified." Brian gently placed his hand on my arm, snapping me back to reality. I shook the thought from my head before speaking.

"I'm fine." A phrase I tended to use when I was anything but fine.

"Are you sure? Because I'm about to ask you a huge favor. But only if you're up for it." Brian knew the things I had experienced, and while we never spoke of it, he was acutely aware of the long-term damage it caused. More so than my husband.

"What can I do to help? I'm sure I'm up for it."

"Can you take the girls home? I literally have a guy who was driving drunk sitting in the back seat of my patrol car. I need some time to manage things at the station."

"Of course. Don't worry about it. We'll figure out dinner and get to bed early."

"I'll stop by the winery and get them on the way home."

"No, we'll go to your house," I said while rubbing the tight muscles on the back of my neck, attempting to knead the stress away. "The girls need a good night's sleep after today's events and all of their things are at home."

Brian leaned over and gave me a quick peck on the cheek. He rarely did this and I always took it as a sign of exceptional gratitude. "Thanks. I'll be home as soon as I can."

"Finish your shift. We'll be fine," I said as the girls moved in next to me.

"I guess I should stop in and see Mrs. Whitmore before I head out," he said after giving the girls goodbye hugs.

When we arrived at Brian's house, the girls went up to change out of the plaid skirts and white button-down collar shirts that were their school uniforms and into pajama pants and t-shirts. While they changed, I texted Edward.

A change in evening plans. Come to Brian's house. I'll explain later. Bring Pizza!

As they finished their homework, I glanced out the window, noticing it was nearly sundown. I stood up without giving it any thought and began closing the blinds and drapes around the house. While I did, the doorbell rang. I checked the peephole and opened the door. The girls raced to it, all but pushing me out of the way.

"Uncle Edward!" They squealed as they hugged him and he flashed me one of his gorgeous smiles. "You brought pizza! And soda too!"

Brian did not keep soda in the house, so it was always a special treat when they had the chance to have it.

"Aunt Cassie," The girls started calling me Aunt Cassie during the Christmas holiday season and cemented the name after spending a weekend with us at Thomas Hall. "Can we have a picnic in the den and watch a movie?"

Moments later the girls were on a blanket while sitting on the floor eating dinner and watching the 1980's classic film, Footloose. The girls let Edward choose the movie. Why he chose it, I had no idea.

When the movie was done, I made sure backpacks were packed for school and fresh uniforms were pressed and laid out for the morning. I was not their favorite person when I made them complete their chore list. However, I was instantly forgiven when I pulled cookie dough out of the freezer and removed a batch of hot chocolate chip cookies from the oven ten minutes later. After a bedtime snack of milk and cookies, Edward and I sent the girls up to their rooms. Gina and Georgie had separate rooms, but according to Brian, they woke in the same bed every morning.

After the girls were settled in, I walked through the house, carefully tidying up any messes we had made and a few extra messes as well. Brian's house was a traditional cape cod style home. The lawn was well kept and the inside resembled exactly what you'd expect a single father of twin girls' home to look like, chaotic and happy. It had a certain energy that I was looking for in my home. The energy of children. An energy I craved.

Edward followed me into the kitchen, his eyes focused on the back door, slightly ajar. "Was that open like that all night?"

"I'm not sure," I said as I closed the door completely and flipped the deadbolt. I felt my chest tighten. Someone could have gotten in. I looked around the kitchen and over at Edward. Without saying a word, he knew my concern.

"I'll go check on the girls and make sure no one is in here that shouldn't be."

The microwave's clock read nine twenty-three. Brian's shift would not end until ten and I needed something to do while Edward checked out the house. I tidied up the living room, wiped down the kitchen counters, and decided to mop the floor. I was nearly done filling the bucket with hot, soapy water when I heard the back door rattle. The knob rattled again. I held my breath and watched the door handle without blinking. When it rattled a third time I ran into the living room, nearly plowing down Edward in the process.

"Someone's trying to get in the house." I whispered the words so quietly I was surprised he heard me. "The kitchen door."

Edward headed for the kitchen and as he did, I called Brian. I told him about the ajar door and the rattling of the handle as calmly as I possibly could.

"I'm on my way home," was all he said before disconnecting.

I squeezed my phone in my hand and sat on the bottom step. I felt the tightness in my chest as my breathing became erratic. I tried to focus on breathing, hoping not to work myself into a full-blown panic attack. Edward had not yet returned to the living room when I heard the gravel crunch as Brian's patrol car pulled into the driveway and saw the brightness of his flashlight as he began to search the perimeter. The light stopped moving, turned off, and I heard Brian and Edward's voices. A woman's voice mingled with theirs. The talking stopped and my phone vibrated. It was a text from Brian.

Open the front door. Everything is fine.

Chapter Twelve

I OPENED THE DOOR and Edward stepped over the threshold and headed toward the sofa but did not sit. Brian was right behind him. The woman followed them into the house like she owned the place. She did not bother to close the door and I could still smell the stale odor of cigarette smoke. Upon seeing me she stopped.

"Oh," she said with a smirk, but not before cementing her eyes on me and taking a long stare. "I think there's a situation here. Who are you?"

I had never seen this woman before in my life. Willow Creek was a small town. I thought I knew, or at least had seen, most everyone in it. Her long hair and striking features would have been something I remembered. Because, aside from the eye color, she looked incredibly like me. We were both about five foot seven, with dark hair, fair skin, and curvy. This woman was a little larger through the hips and slightly less busty. Even those differences were so subtle that if I had not been born with green eyes, we would have been near mirror images of one another. We locked eyes, seeing the baffled expression on each other's faces. We both stood motionless for a moment before simultaneously breaking our connection.

"Cassandra Baker."

"Baker, huh?"

"And you are?" I asked. I did not even know her name yet but something about her voice and personality was distasteful and unsettling. The last time I felt this way was with Henry's late wife, Darla, and she tried to kill me a couple of times. My first instinct was that this woman had to go. Be it by leaving town or leaving the living.

She paused before answering, looking me up and down. It was only then I realized I was barefoot, still in yoga pants, tank top, and cardigan.

"I'm Brian's wife, Stefanie Hayes."

"Ex-wife. Our divorce has been final for a few years now."

"You divorced me?" Her voice cracked with fake disappointment.

This was a conversation I did not need to be present for. I decided to go check on the girls and make sure their doors were closed. I started up the stairs when I heard her say, "I want to see the twins."

I turned back around, standing on the third step, blocking the staircase. Brian looked distraught by the thought. I did not wait for him to speak to her but interjected myself back into the conversation.

"They're asleep. They have school tomorrow. And I think they should be told you're back before they see you."

"Who gave you permission to make that decision, Miss Baker?" Stefanie asked indignantly.

"It's *Mrs.* Baker," Edward said as he made his way through the room to me. He wrapped his arms low around my waist and I closed my eyes for a brief moment and melted. The day was catching up with me fast. "Stefanie, where the hell have you been?"

The look on her face told me she knew Edward well. Very well. I knew my husband was no monk before we met and my intuition told me this woman had spent time in my husband's bed. And I did not like it. However, I was more determined to protect the girls from what would be undoubtedly a traumatic reunion than discuss my husband's sexual history with a stranger.

"Ms. Hayes, tell me something. What's the name of Gina's best friend?"

Her response was a blank stare.

"Okay, how about this? Tell me the name of Georgie's boyfriend."

Her expression didn't change except to blink, but Brian looked at me with an expression that bordered terror. "She has a boyfriend?"

"It's nothing serious. Just some handholding. We'll talk later," I said before redirecting my attention back to Stefanie, while still being held by Edward. "As for you, you don't know these girls well enough to upend their world on a Wednesday night. Especially since they have a history test in the morning."

"And you think you're going to stop me?"

I was not one to pick a fight, but my overprotectiveness of the twins kicked in fast. I stared her down, determined not to blink first. "Put your foot on the first step of this staircase and find out."

Edward dropped his arms, and while I didn't look at him, I knew he was dumbfounded by my response as he had never heard me threaten violence before. She took two steps in the direction of the staircase before Brian blocked her progress.

"Okay, ladies. That's enough for tonight." Brian was determined to end things before someone got arrested. As he spoke, I heard the footsteps of one of the girls walking toward the bathroom.

"Look, Brian. You can do whatever you want concerning the girls," I said, pointedly ignoring Stefanie. "They're your children. But tonight, don't tell them."

"Cassandra, you're right. Not tonight. It's late. Stef, let's talk on the porch swing outside."

The two walked out of the house but not before she side-eyed me and mumbled, "This isn't over yet, Bitch."

Edward and I moved to the living room sofa. I leaned into him and he draped his arm around me.

"So, you haven't had a chance to tell me, how did you end up here?"

Edward was trying to be nonchalant, but mild agitation seeped through his voice. Edward and Brian had a strained relationship long before I met either of them. I am certain he was not happy to discover me in Brian's house barefoot and in yoga clothes when he arrived earlier in the evening but wasn't going to say anything in front of the twins.

I recounted the events of the afternoon from start to finish, leaving out the mild panic attack in the emergency room lobby. When I was done, my husband's only response was, "You've had a full day, haven't you?"

He kissed me on the forehead and smiled. There was a pause in our conversation and we could hear raised voices outside.

"I have to say what I saw on the staircase earlier was a side of you I've never seen."

"What do you mean?"

"Let me quote you. 'Put your foot on the first step of this staircase and find out'," he smirked. "What were you going to do?"

"Truthfully, I have no idea." I quietly laughed at myself. Had I really said that? "She wasn't going to get up those stairs though. Not tonight."

Edward cupped my face in his hands. "You are incredible, Sweetie. Those girls are blessed to have you in their lives. I've never known anyone as fiercely protective of children as you. Even when they aren't yours."

"You know how I feel about children. I don't envy Brian though. He's going to have to tell them tomorrow. But I guess that's not truly our problem to solve." I paused, considering how to move the conversation along. There was no good way to do it, so I just asked my next question. "Stefanie looked like she knew you very well. Care to elaborate?"

Edward hesitated before he spoke. "It's a small town. I spent a lot of time in Willow Creek when I was younger. You get to know everybody."

A gut feeling told me he was not being honest, again. I wanted to call him out on not disclosing more about his relationship with Stefanie, but I was tired. Too tired to bother digging up the past. I closed my eyes and took a deep breath. Before I could say anymore, Edward's phone rang. As he answered it, Brian entered the house alone. He appeared stressed and teary-eyed.

Edward was intensely concentrating on whatever the person on the other end of the line had to say. Even when Edward was not at work, he was at work. I got up and went into the kitchen to find Brian unloading the dishwasher. I sat on one of the 1950's style diner chairs.

"Hell of a day, huh?" He commented.

"Where's your head, Brian?" I always thought it was an unusual expression, but it was the perfect question for this situation.

"I'm not sure. There's a lot for me to process."

"Same here." Brian looked confused so I continued, elaborating on the statement. "Were you ever planning on mentioning that I look almost exactly like your ex-wife?"

"I thought I would never see her again and you'd never meet her. So, what would have been the point?" I was not certain how I felt about that statement, and it created more questions in my mind that I was too tired to address. I yawned and rubbed my eyes. When I did not comment, Brian changed the subject and continued speaking. "Thanks for stepping in and looking out for the girls' best interests. Thoughts on how to handle this with them?"

I paused before answering, giving myself a minute to think it through. "Let them get through school tomorrow. Tell them after school and have them spend the evening processing it before they meet with her. But only if they want to. Don't push them. It will only make things worse. Don't plan on them going to school Friday. They're at a tough age. They'll need the weekend to process it."

"Will you be around?"

"I think so. Brian, should I give them their birthday presents early? I'm thinking it might be a good idea."

"What did you get them?" Edward asked as he entered the room.

"Cell Phones. But I asked Brian first."

"Yeah. I think it's a bit much, but they really want them and Cassandra offered." Brian shook his head as he spoke. "Thirteen on Monday. How did that happen so quickly?"

The two men stared at each other. It was as if they were sharing a memory. I could not tell you any more than that as their expressions were blank. After a moment, Edward looked away from Brian and focused his attention on me.

"I guess we should get out of here. I'm sure we are all exhausted." Edward was right. It had been a long day for me and the panic from what I thought was an attempted break-in had sucked what little energy I had left out of my body.

As he was speaking, I turned to get my purse and found Georgie standing in the doorway. She walked over to me in a sleepy daze.

"What's the matter?" I asked.

"I just had the strangest dream. When I woke up, I was thirsty, so I came down for some water. You're going home?" She asked sleepily as she hugged me and then Edward.

Brian cringed. The two men hadn't gotten along well long before I arrived at Thomas Hall. They tried to be civil toward each other since I was married to one of them and best friends with the other. However, as time passed, their relationship grew more strained. While Edward and I talked to the very sleepy pre-teen, Brian fixed her a glass of ice water. I took it from him and looked at the two men.

"I'll walk back up with her. Try to play nice."

As we made our way up the stairs, I asked Georgie about her dream.

"I dreamt my mother was here, in the house, with us. Like living here. It seemed so real."

"Do you have that dream often?" I asked. Already beginning to worry about the weekend and the events to come.

"Sometimes. I don't really remember her or what she looked like, but I sometimes dream about her."

"I understand. After my mom died, I would dream of her too." It was somewhat true. I really did not remember my dreams, but I still had nightmares of the car accident that killed her and my father when I was young. They were visions that woke me in tears.

"Do you think my mom is dead?" Georgie asked, sounding terrified.

"Oh no. I am absolutely certain she is alive." I quickly reassured her. "I just understand the dreaming part. It always seems so real, doesn't it? You should get some sleep. Tomorrow is a busy day."

She was already back in bed, having sipped some of her water, and placed the cup on the bedside table. I stood up to walk out of the room when Georgie spoke. "Aunt Cassie, thanks for coming tonight. Something strange is brewing around here. Like grandma says, I can feel it in my bones."

By the time Edward and I got back to Thomas Hall, it was nearly midnight. Edward drove my sky blue Volkswagen Beetle, which he hated, but had no choice since he sent his driver home hours earlier. It was a quiet trip home. In the darkness, it was difficult to tell if Edward was tired or upset with me for some reason. He usually talked the entire time he drove us somewhere. He liked the fact that I was trapped in a vehicle with him and could not avoid whatever topic he wanted to discuss. However, there was complete silence in the car as we made the trip home. Even the radio was off.

Upon arriving home though, we immediately climbed into bed, not even bothering to change clothes, and fell asleep spooned together within seconds. I was so tired I didn't feel him kiss me the next morning when he left for work.

Chapter Thirteen

I WAS EATING MY usual breakfast of toast with strawberry jam and hot tea when I had a thought. I picked up the phone and dialed.

"Saint Margaret's Academy. This is Mrs. Price. How may I help you?"

"Good morning. My name is Cassandra Baker. I'm calling on behalf of the Hayes twins."

"Ah, Regina and Georgia. Delightful, intelligent girls."

"I don't know if their father has called this morning, but it is imperative that no one pick up the girls today unless their father is called first. Even if they are on the pre-approved list."

"Mrs. Baker, is there a problem?" Mrs. Price, the school secretary, sounded concerned.

"I'm sure you are aware of Mr. Hayes's job. I might be overreacting but there's a safety concern today that normally doesn't exist." I was not about to tell the school that the safety concern was the twins' own mother. "They are perfectly safe at school as long as they remain there."

"Could you hold a moment please?"

I waited patiently and within a few minutes, I was speaking with the principal.

"Mrs. Baker, we will keep a close eye on the girls. They normally take the bus home after school. Should they do that today?"

I made a quick decision. "No, have them go to the office at the end of the day. I'll meet them there. I'll get Brian to call you and confirm it. Thank you so much for your assistance with this matter."

"Not a problem. And Mrs. Baker, please thank your husband again for his generous donation last month in addition to the girls' tuitions for next year."

We said our goodbyes and hung up. I was not aware Edward donated to Saint Margaret's Academy, let alone paid the tuition for the twins. It was obvious to me though why he had chosen to do this. Early on, Edward told me about the only serious relationship he ever had but only gave me an overview. Later, when it came up again, I thought that I had been told the whole story. However, it appeared, that I had not. He told me the woman had children from another relationship and felt that seeing her children get a good education was his penance for the mistakes he made during their relationship. It was only now that I understood the children were Georgie and Gina and the person he was involved with was Stefanie. It explained a little more of the strained relationships that Edward, Brian, and Stefanie had with one another but I still had more questions than answers.

After I was dressed and ready to leave the house, I realized I had not cleared any of this with Brian. His phone went straight to voicemail, so I left him a lengthy message explaining myself. I told him if I had overstepped my bounds to call me.

I wandered over to my office, a short walk down the path from our home at Thomas Hall. I was in no hurry. There wasn't much for me to do. When I first took over the operation of the winery, I ran around like a chicken with my head cut off. After solving a distribution issue, updating the winery's computer system, and taking a full inventory the winery ran itself for the most part. Everyone had a job to do at the winery and my position had last been held by a retired gentleman who considered this a hobby.

After arriving, I made myself a cup of hot tea and sat in my usual spot on the sofa that overlooked the vines through the largest window in the room. It was mid-May and a cool morning, but the vines looked glorious. I had just taken the last sip of my ginger peach tea when Alex tapped on the door frame before walking in.

"Are you ready to do this?" Alex asked as he made himself a cup of coffee, turned a chair from next to my desk toward me, and sat.

"Do you wish you had never agreed to this?" When I first took over the winery he agreed to advise and guide me on the inner workings of the winery and the schedule for everything that happens.

"You know I don't mind. Things are quiet right now for the winery but as the month goes on, it's going to get busier in the vineyard. We'll be out in the fields more often than not." He handed me an outline he created for the next month. He did this for every meeting and I used it as a guide as the month progressed. We had just begun to dig into the outline when my phone rang.

"Cassandra Baker."

"Thank you." It was Brian's baritone voice, but it sounded more stressed than it had in quite some time, maybe the most stressed since we met.

"You're welcome. But for what?"

"I just got a call from the school. Stefanie tried to pick up the girls from St. Margaret's. When they refused, in large part because of your phone call, she made a scene and the secretary called the station. Two officers just escorted her off the property."

"Hold on a second."

"Alex, can we finish this later? I think this might take a while and I know you've got a busy day. I don't want to waste your time."

Alex nodded his head and smiled, poured another cup of coffee, and headed out my office door.

My first thought was about how mortifying this was for the girls. The embarrassment must have been horrible. My heart ached for them. This woman seemed to be an expert at hurting her children. While they were not old enough to remember her, I had seen signs of abandonment issues in the two girls. They were both people pleasers but weren't trusting of most of the adults. I tamped down my anger so I could be of help to them.

"Maybe I should go pick up the girls for you. They aren't going to want to be at school after that outburst."

"Great minds think alike. Are you up for playing the cool aunt two days in a row?"

I paused, not answering the question but asking one instead. "Do you mind if the girls stay here tonight? It would give you time to sort things out with Stefanie and they would give me some company. Edward has to fly to Atlanta after work." Brian was unaware that I had spent most nights alone over the last couple of months.

"Actually, that would be great. I'm supposed to meet with her after work. I'd prefer not to do it in public, but I didn't want it to be in the house with the girls."

"Well, keep me posted with what's going on. I'll leave work and go get the girls now." I was already halfway down the path when I said it.

When I got to the house, I caught a glimpse of myself in the mirror. The Thomas Hall t-shirt, jeans, ponytail, and windbreaker would not do today. I needed to look like a woman whose children, or at least nieces, belonged at Saint Margaret's Academy. I changed into gray slacks, a V-necked, black blouse, put on a little makeup, added jewelry, and changed out tennis shoes for a pair of black pumps. After fiddling with my hair, I settled on a half-up, half-down style that looked every day but upscale. I was only home for twenty minutes before the car arrived at the house and I was ready to go. I rarely used any of the limos, but I thought it would be a nice treat for the girls. It also made an impression.

When I arrived at the school, the girls were already waiting for me in the office. Brian had called ahead to let them know I was en route. The office was bright with fluorescent lights, but the walls were painted a lovely sandy color. Cushioned armchairs and a blue sofa lined one wall and two copying machines were pushed against the other available wall. The secretary's desk consisted of a low cherrywood counter filled with paper forms, iPads, and laptops. The two girls huddled together on the sofa of the waiting area, whispering back and forth between sobs. My heart ached for them. As I watched them an older woman in a suit approached me.

"Mrs. Baker?" She asked.

"Yes." The girls heard my voice and turned their attention away from each other and focused their tear-stained eyes on me for a split second before dropping their heads back into their huddle.

"I'm Mrs. Wilson, the principal." Mrs. Wilson was a short, plump woman with silvery-white hair pulled into a severe bun. She wore a navy suit and a white blouse. The jacket, while she was able to get it on, wasn't quite large enough and the buttons pulled under the strain. She carried herself in a refined manner that hinted at wealth and position. She shook my hand as she spoke. "Thank you for arriving so quickly."

"Excuse me for one moment." I walked away from her and knelt in front of the girls who held each other's hands in comfort. Their heads were down, hair falling in their faces like curtains, hiding their eyes.

"Hey. Look at me." I placed a hand on each of the girls' knees before I whispered quietly and calmly as they looked up. "It's going to be okay. We'll get through this. I promise. The limo and driver are out front. Why don't y'all go hop in and I'll be there in a few minutes. There's soda and juice in the fridge." The two girls peered out the window and smiled when they saw the black stretch limo. The tears subsided and they headed to the car but not before giving me a hug. I turned my attention back to Mrs. Wilson. "My apologies. I just couldn't stand to see them in such a state."

Mrs. Wilson smiled. "You love them very much, don't you?"

"They remind me of everything that's important. Maybe someday Edward and I will send our children here. You have a lovely school." I was obsessed with starting a family and had been since before we were married. Edward was happy to play his part when he made his way home.

"I just need you to sign them out and you'll be all set." As we walked to the counter, I could not help but notice Mrs. Wilson staring at me. Once she realized I was aware of her gaze, she continued speaking. "I'm sorry, Mrs. Baker. I was unaware that you were related to the girls and their mother."

"I'm not. I'm just a friend of Brian's."

"Wow! The resemblance is remarkable. Striking actually."

Mrs. Wilson's words took me back to what the emergency room doctor said regarding the resemblance of the girls to me. He used almost the exact same words. It stirred up thoughts in my head about a time when Brian expressed an interest in me beyond friendship and created new questions in my mind. As quickly as the thoughts entered my head, I shook them out.

I signed the appropriate forms and made my way back to the car.

It was past four in the afternoon before we arrived back at Thomas Hall. As we pulled up to the house, I realized I had yet to give the girls their birthday gifts. We made our way in, lugging in shopping bags from Zoe's Boutique.

Zoe Marshall was the owner of the best boutique and day spa in town and the girlfriend of my brother-in-law, Henry. I met Zoe the first weekend I arrived at Thomas Hall and from the moment we shook hands she had been the best of allies. She was exotically beautiful with long, straight black hair and flawless caramel skin.

She was a dear friend, not just to me, but to the entire Baker family as well.

When we walked into her shop, we were the only people in the store. Zoe was hanging a new shipment of shorts to be displayed.

"Hey ladies," she said, looking at me, the twins, and then back at me, slightly confused.

"We are in the middle of a retail therapy crisis." I fished an American Express Black card from my purse and slapped it onto the counter. She picked it up and tried to hand it back to me. My husband was a silent partner in her business but she was in the process of buying him out. "No Zoe, you need to charge me today. We're about to do some serious shopping. What do you have that will fit these two? Summer's coming and I know they've grown. They are both an inch taller than they were at Christmas."

She immediately began scurrying from rack to rack pulling items and asking the girls questions about colors and preferred cuts of clothing. After we sent them off to the fitting rooms, Zoe turned to me. "What's going on?"

"Their mom showed up at school earlier today and made a scene."

"Holy shit!"

"I couldn't agree more. They haven't said much about it yet, but the girls have got to be devastated. I didn't know what else to do with them, so I figured we would start here. Any clue on how to amuse two heartbroken teenage girls for twenty-four hours?"

"I don't know but let's start by spoiling the hell out of them here." Zoe walked over to the fitting rooms and knocked on the doors. "Let's see these outfits ladies. Pedicures and manicures await. Both of you need a trim too. Your bangs are getting too long."

Zoe's spent a large part of the afternoon playing the part of sassy stylist to the twins. She was basically being herself, only slightly more exaggerated. She ordered in sandwiches for lunch and sent one of her stylists to other stores to find things for the girls that she did not have in a small enough size. When we left, they each had a few new outfits, cobalt blue toenails and fingernails, with matching blue extensions in their hair. I was certain Brian would have something to say about the hair.

The driver followed us into my house with carry-out boxes of various dishes from my favorite Italian restaurant, Casa de Mimmo's. Exhausted, we all dropped onto sofas and chairs. I looked at the girls and said, "It's time for birthday presents."

"But Aunt Cassie, our birthday is still four days away."

"And I thought all of this was our birthday present," Gina commented.

"This was just a little fun, but I want you to have your birthday gifts now."

I went into my bedroom, retrieving two boxes with cards attached by ribbons from the top of my dresser. I handed them to the girls. Each girl read their card, thanking me before even unwrapping the boxes.

"Oh. My. God!" Gina screamed.

"No way!" Georgie whispered.

I could feel my smile grow as I watched them take their phones out of the boxes.

"I downloaded a few apps and added a bunch of numbers in the contacts for you. Of course, you are free to add whatever you want, they're yours."

Suddenly, the girls looked at one another.

"Aunt Cassie, we can't accept these," Georgie said, placing the phone gently back in the box. "The thought is super cool, but I don't think Dad can afford the monthly service for both of us."

"That's not his problem. Edward and I will be paying the monthly bill until you graduate from high school. However, if your grades go south or you start getting in trouble, I will shut them down. Understand?"

"Yes, Ma'am." They said in unison, grinning from ear to ear.

The remainder of the evening was spent eating Italian food, watching videos on YouTube and TikTok, giving a fashion show of the new clothes I bought them, and of course, playing on their cell phones. I had the girls send selfies to Edward showing off their new hairstyles. He sent the girls smiley faces and me a text.

Brian's going to kill you.

It was almost nine when my phone rang. I nearly missed the call as the latest K-Pop group's music was blasting through the speakers in the house.

"Cassandra Baker."

"I hope so," Edward said, laughing as he spoke. "But I can barely hear you. Throwing a party?"

I laughed with him as I walked onto the back patio, closing the door behind me. A warm breeze blew my hair around my face.

"Yes, I'm partying hard with two nearly thirteen-year-old girls with blue hair extensions. How was your day?"

"Long, and still not over. Right now, I'm flying to Atlanta for that early morning meeting. Did Brian really agree to the hair or did you make an executive decision?"

The volume of giggling girls overtook the sound of the music. I sat in one of the patio chairs and continued my conversation with Edward.

"I let the girls make that call. When are you coming home?" I rarely asked but decided I needed to do it more, if for no other reason than to remind him where home was. It was with me.

"Tomorrow afternoon. I need to swing by the office for a while before heading to the winery." He paused for a moment, changing the subject. He must have known I was wondering if I would even see him this weekend. Once he walked into his office, he had trouble leaving it. However, he chose not to comment and continued on to a different topic. "How late are the girls staying tonight?"

"They're here for the night. Brian and Stefanie need to hash things out. I thought it would be better for the girls to be elsewhere."

"Probably a good idea."

"You won't believe what Stefanie did today. She showed up at St. Margaret's."

"Oh, God." As he spoke, the signal began to break up. I heard him say Stefanie's name and something about Brian but could not make out the rest.

"Edward? You're breaking up. Can you hear me?"

And then he was gone. I sat for a moment reflecting on how much this conversation mirrored our current lives. Me here, him working somewhere that wasn't here. Short phone calls and never enough time to really talk. "Maybe," I said to myself, "things will change. I know he's trying."

I went back in, fixed everyone a bowl of rocky road ice cream, and turned down the music as I walked into the room. "Okay ladies. It's time to get serious. I know you didn't want to talk about everything when I picked you up, but I think it's time."

Gina immediately became tense and defensive. "I don't understand how our mother just showed up at school this morning. Somebody had to know she was in town."

"I'm going to tell you something, but I want you to listen to everything I have to say before you respond." I took a deep breath and sighed. "Your mother showed up at your dad's house around ten last night asking to see you. Your dad was going to tell you after school today. We had no idea she'd show up at St. Margaret's."

"She was at the house last night?" Georgie asked.

"She was. And I suggested to your father to wait until he had a chance to tell you about her return. I guess it wasn't the greatest idea. I just wanted you to be in the best position possible to handle the news. I knew it would be traumatizing."

Gina's face was beet red and her teeth clenched, but Georgie's expression was more reflective.

"I don't think you were wrong," Georgie said. I could tell she was about to choose her words carefully. "We don't know her. Where has she been? What has she been doing all of this time? Why did she come back now?"

As Georgie asked questions, Gina's hot-headed expression continued to plaster her face. I was certain the anger was directed at me until she spoke. "Georgie's right. We don't know her. And I don't think I want to know her either."

Chapter Fourteen

Friday evening found Edward and I snuggled up on the sofa watching *Cleopatra*. As comfortable as it seemed, tension still lingered in the air, a tiny remnant of the last two weeks. He may have been watching the movie, but I was deep in thought. Usually, we would talk about other things while watching an old movie, but not on this particular evening. There were too many things racing through my head. Just about the time Elizabeth Taylor was rolled out of the carpet, Edward turned off the television.

"What's wrong?" He asked.

"What do you mean?" There were several things on my mind but none I felt like discussing.

"You're quiet tonight. Too quiet. It's making me nervous."

"I'm sorry. I've just got a lot on my mind." He took my hand, looking to be reassured.

"The twins? Was Brian mad about the blue hair?"

"Surprisingly, no. He has so many other things to worry about right now that he hasn't said a word about it. The whole thing with the vines has me distracted. It's just so bizarre." There were even more things on my mind, not all of which I was ready to say out loud. A knock on the front door granted me a reprieve.

Edward walked over and swung open the heavy oak door to find Stefanie standing on our porch. She was wearing a skin-tight red dress that barely held her breasts in place along with three inch heels. The dress was at least a size too small and the clingy material did her no favors.

"Stef, what are you doing here?"

"I thought you might want to spend the night with a real woman and not some little girl."

I felt my face get blisteringly hot. Edward ignored the comment and asked another question. "And how the hell did you get past the guards at the gate?"

He had not finished his second question before she walked in, ignored me, sat down, and made herself at home in the oversized chair. And that moment confirmed everything I thought at Brian's house. Everything made sense. Stefanie was the reason Edward and Brian didn't get along. I was certain of it. I just wished the two of us did not look so much alike. But then again, maybe that was part of the issue with Brian and Edward where I was concerned.

"I missed you. I've thought about you a lot over the last ten years."

"It sounds like the two of you need a few minutes," I said, assertively inserting myself into the conversation. "Why don't I get everyone a drink?" I turned to Stefanie as I stood. "Ms. Hayes? Would you like a glass of wine? Soda? Tea? Water?"

"Wine is fine, but I'd rather have a beer if you've got one."

I walked past the spot to where Edward had relocated himself, still standing. He stopped me as I reached him, hooked an arm loosely around my waist, pulled me close, and planted a long, lingering kiss on my lips. When he finished, I smiled and continued toward the kitchen. He was trying to make a point to Stefanie and I appreciated the effort.

I listened to the conversation unfold in the next room as I opened a beer and filled the frosted glass I had pulled from the freezer, poured Edward a bourbon on the rocks, and a glass of iced tea for me. I arranged them on a tray with a bowl of cheese straws and a few napkins.

"Did ya miss me?" She asked Edward.

"You met my wife. That should answer your question."

"God, Edward, she's a child." My jaw clenched and I forced myself not to grind my teeth.

"She may be young, but she's no child. And she's what I waited for my entire life." I smiled, although my jaw muscles remained tight.

"I thought that was me. Is that why you married her? Because she looks like me? The resemblance is uncanny."

"Really? I never noticed," Edward said. "And you never answered my question. What are you doing here?"

I listened to Edward speak as I returned from the kitchen, set the tray on the coffee table, and took a seat on the sofa next to Edward. I handed him his drink and put my hand on his thigh as he took a large gulp.

Stef turned her attention to me. I do not know if she expected me to say something, but I made up my mind to avoid engaging or being provoked by this woman if at all possible. This was my house and I was not going to let her push my buttons. She stared at me for what seemed like an exceptionally long moment.

"I'm beginning to wonder if you own anything besides yoga pants."

I looked down at what I was wearing. "You didn't come here to discuss my wardrobe. So, whatever you came to say, say it. My husband and I have plans this evening that don't include you."

"You are correct. I really don't care what you're wearing." She turned and made eye contact with Edward. "To answer your question, I came back to connect with my girls and try to rebuild my life. I was hoping to rekindle my relationship with you too."

I glared at Stefanie, uncertain if I was going to punch her or walk out of the room. No one had ever brought out violent tendencies in me the way she did, and, if I heard her correctly, she had just propositioned my husband twice in a matter of a few minutes as well. In front of me! In my house! Edward heard the low growl I was trying to suppress as I balled the hand on his thigh into a fist. I looked at him and saw his soft, sexy eyes lovingly staring at me and ignoring Stefanie. I took a deep breath and regained control of myself.

"Stefanie, I'm a happily married man and you're embarrassing yourself."

I stood and faced Edward, my back to her, blocking her from being part of our conversation. "Honey, I'm going to let you handle this while I go for a walk." I pivoted to Edward's side, giving her a full view of me grabbing the collar of his shirt and pulling him to me so I could plant my lips against his mouth. I held the kiss until my thoughts began to include stripping his clothes off.

"Sweetie, where are you walking to? I worry when I don't know where you are."

"I know you do," I said sweetly even though it irritated me that he was still trying to maintain control over my movement. However, it was not the time to discuss it. I wanted Stefanie to see no cracks in our relationship that she thought she could use to wedge her way back into my husband's world. I chose my words carefully, for maximum effect even though they were only half-true. "I'm going up to Mom's house for a bit. The chef is testing out a new cookie recipe tonight for when the twins next visit. I think I'll go steal some."

"Bring me back a few." I could tell he was uncertain as to whether I was telling the truth or making the whole thing up but was willing to play along.

I squeezed his hand and he lifted mine to his lips and let them slowly graze across my knuckles as the corners of his mouth turned upward. I made my way to the door, grabbed my phone off the desk, and slipped on my flip-flops. As I left, I heard Edward say, "You are not a part of my life anymore. In case I haven't been clear, let me spell it out for you, I don't want you here and neither does my wife."

He continued to speak but his voice faded as I walked away. His voice sounded so sexy and I loved the words coming out of his mouth. I would have to thank him properly after that woman was off the property. I closed my eyes for a moment, contemplating exactly how I would thank him, and grinned.

I opened my eyes to a rapidly approaching storm and saw the first bolt of lightning as I dialed Brian's number.

"Hey."

"You're not going to believe this," I replied, not even saying hello. "Stefanie is at Thomas Hall."

"Have you killed her yet? I really thought you were contemplating it the other night at my house."

"I left the house in order to avoid just that. She had the nerve to proposition my husband in front of me. Brian, how did she get on the property? We got no call from the gate tonight. She must have known another way in. I think she may know a lot of things I don't."

"Huh," Brian said, and then went silent as though he could read my thoughts.

"So, you're not going to fill me in on this love triangle either?"

"How did you know?"

"It's obvious and explains a lot. It would have been nice to know sooner though."

"Cassandra, I can't talk about it. She broke my heart and then disappeared. The day she dropped the kids off for the weekend, she told me things that destroyed me. I..., I... just can't."

Brian's voice dropped off. As much as I wanted to press him for information and as much as I knew he would tell me if I forced the subject, I let the conversation end. I hated to see a friend in pain. As we said our goodbyes, the rain began to fall and by the time I reached the front door of the main house I was soaking wet. I let myself in and found Vivian and Poppy sitting in the library, drinking coffee, and chatting.

"You're back!" I said, hugging them both while trying not to get them wet. "I didn't think you were home for a few more days. How was Aruba?"

"Glorious," Vivian said. "But dear, what are you doing out in this storm? You are soaked to the bone."

"I'm just going to say one name. Stefanie Hayes."

"Stefanie? She's back?" She tilted her face to the ceiling and rolled her eyes in an un-Vivian-like fashion. "Cassandra, she's a viper. Someone not to be trifled with. We need to get rid of her as soon as possible."

I was pretty sure that Vivian was saying "get rid of her" in the literal sense. She had dealt with someone in such a way before and I knew she would do it again, especially if it was to protect me.

"Where is she now?" She asked.

"At the house with Edward." Vivian looked at Poppy, shook her head, and exhaled hard.

Poppy began to speak when my cell phone rang. It was Brian.

"I was just waved through at the gate. Where should I go?"

"Wherever you think is best. Stefanie and Edward are at my house. I'm at the main."

"Why did you think it was a wise move to leave the two of them alone?"

"Because I didn't want you to have to arrest me tonight. I don't think I could list all the reasons why, but that woman infuriates me. Maybe I should've just killed her when I had the chance at your house."

"Cassandra!" Poppy exclaimed, never having heard me say anything like that before.

"I think I'm going to start at your house. You might see me at the main house too if that's okay."

"Sure, but full disclosure. Poppy's here."

"Okay."

Poppy and Brian's paths rarely crossed and when they did it was because of me. I tried my best not to put them in awkward situations by letting them both know if the other was present prior to their arrival.

I hung up the phone and placed the palms of my hands against my now throbbing temples. Vivian came to where I was standing and put a hand on my shoulder. "Why don't you go up and change into some dry clothes and I'll have someone bring you something for your headache."

I silently made my way towards the staircase, heading in the direction of Edward's childhood suite, stopping only along the way to kiss Poppy on the cheek. As I climbed the stairs, I heard Poppy say, "When is that poor child ever going to catch a break?"

The Edward Suite was, as the name implies, Edward's room. He spent what seemed to be a happy childhood there. The layout was similar to other suites in the house. A sitting room, bedroom, bathroom, and a walk-in closet. The only difference was that there was only a half wall between the sitting room, which Edward had used as a video game room, and the bedroom. This made the bed visible from the door.

I went into the walk-in closet to see what of mine was hanging up in there. Somehow, over time, various pieces of my clothing ended up at the main house. I found a red fitted V-necked shirt, khaki capris, and a pair of black flats I had been looking for. I took advantage of the fact that the suite's bathroom was attached to the closet. I washed my face and brushed my still wet hair pulling it up into a ponytail. I had just finished pulling my hair back when there was a knock on the door. Before I could answer it, Vivian came in with Tylenol for my headache.

"Thank you," I said, opening the bottle and downing two with no water.

"Are you okay?"

"That's a loaded question. I'm not sure I can answer it."

There was a pause in the conversation. Not uncomfortable in length, but more of a hesitation on Vivian's part.

"Cassandra, do you know Stefanie and Edward's history?"

"I've never been told, but I'm beginning to have a good idea of what that story looks like."

"Tell me what you're thinking and I'll tell you if you're right," she said as she gently sat on the sofa in the sitting area.

"Well," I paused, turning to look at her. "Wait, what about Poppy? Is he downstairs alone? The last thing I would want to do is be disrespectful."

She smiled and shook her head. "Always thinking about everyone but yourself. He's fine. After you headed up here, he got a phone call and is in the study attending to his business."

I wondered what Vivian thought about Poppy's line of work, but I did not want to appear to be avoiding her request, so I tabled that question for the moment.

"Well, here's how I think this played out." I said, sitting down next to her. "Stefanie and Edward were an item. Then Stefanie and Brian started dating. Or the other way around. I'm not sure about the timing of it all. And when she got pregnant with the twins, she didn't know who the father was."

"You've pretty much nailed it. Do you want me to tell you the rest?"

"No. I'll wait for Edward to tell me. I think I need to hear it from him."

"Fair enough. We should probably go downstairs and see what's going on."

We made our way downstairs, only to find Poppy finishing his phone call. Almost immediately his phone rang again. He looked at the caller ID. For a moment, I could have sworn he rolled his eyes.

"Good evening, Isabella. What can I do for you tonight?"

I could not make out what she was saying, but her voice carried through the phone and into the room. And then, before Poppy could say anything, she hung up the phone.

"What was that about?" Vivian asked.

I knew this scene too well. I avoided Isabella Martin like a contagious disease. She was the epitome of a spoiled Italian American Princess and was certain that everyone else on the planet existed solely for granting her wishes. Her brother had the same sense of entitlement and their father, Robert Martin, had encouraged it.

"That granddaughter of mine," Poppy began while shaking his head. "She's angry because she wants to take over the family business and I am not in agreement."

"You got all of that out of a fifteen-second phone call?" I inquired.

"No, I have been getting several calls today from other members of the organization. She has been out of prison for six months and she thinks she can waltz in and take over."

"Even I know better than that," I said. "Poppy, how did she get out of jail so quickly? She only served ten months of a twelve-year sentence."

"You know that the right dollar amount put in the right hands can get things done."

I didn't want to go back to my house while Stefanie was there, but it was what I needed to do. "Vivian, Poppy, I think I'm going to walk back to our house."

I grabbed an umbrella from the stand next to the door. As I walked down the path my mind wandered to earlier thoughts of stripping my husband naked and pushing him onto our bed. Before I could do that though, I needed to face this woman once and for all.

Before I walked in the door, I stopped at the front porch to shake out and fold up my umbrella. Upon entering, I expected to see three people in my living room but the room was empty. I took off my shoes and curled up on the sofa, drinking the tea I left on the table earlier. I wondered where Edward had gone. I debated on whether to call him but found myself dialing his number. It rang twice before he answered.

"Hey, Sweetie. Where are you?" He asked.

"I was going to ask you the same question."

"I drove Stefanie to the place she's staying in town. I'm on my way home now."

I could feel anger building inside of me, so I hung up the phone. I could not believe he was catering to her. I thought he knew how I felt about this woman. If he did not, he was about to find out. I stomped off to our bedroom abandoning any thoughts of sex with my husband. I closed and locked the door before changing into a peach-colored nightgown and climbing into bed.

I heard Edward come into the house and call for me.

I heard him try to open the door only to find it locked.

I heard him knock on the bedroom door.

I heard him say, "Cassie, Sweetie, you accidentally locked me out of the bedroom."

I ignored him.

Chapter Fifteen

I WOKE MUCH EARLIER than I normally did for a Saturday morning after a restless night's sleep. I threw on a robe that matched my nightgown, fixed myself a cup of hot tea, and took it out on the patio, next to the pool. It was only completed a few weeks ago. The water was clear and the rising sun reflected brightly, shimmering off its surface. Within moments, Edward sat down next to me with his cup of coffee.

"Good morning," he began. "I've never been locked out of my own bedroom before."

I said nothing. My parents taught me when I was very young that if you can't say anything nice, don't say anything at all.

"What did I do?" He sounded remorseful, melting away a few layers of my icy exterior but I still was not giving off warm and loving vibes. I took a deep breath and turned to look at him. I could tell by the dark circles under his eyes, that he had not slept much either.

"I was already stressed, and in a mood, last night when Stefanie showed up. I tried to give the two of you the privacy to talk about whatever you needed. But you know how I feel about this woman and then I came home to find you had driven her to town. Couldn't she have ridden with Brian? We have people here who could have driven her home. Why did *you* have to do it?"

"Yeah, you're right. I guess she could have ridden with Brian but he left before she did. Things like that don't usually phase you. You said you were already on edge. Talk to me."

"I'm not sure what to say. That's why I haven't said anything." He reached over and took my hand that lay on the table. I expected him to say something, but he remained silent.

"It's just that I'm pretty sure…" I let my voice fade out.

"Pretty sure of what, Beautiful?"

I shook my head. I knew what I wanted to tell him but was not ready to say it until I was absolutely certain. I stood up, still holding Edward's hand.

"I need more tea. And maybe to crawl back into bed. Want to join me?"

He stood and walked with me into the kitchen. We both refilled our drinks and took them to bed with us.

I don't remember closing my eyes, but when I reopened them, my tea sat on the nightstand, cold, and it was four hours later. I rolled over to discover I was alone.

As I walked into the kitchen, the pink roses on the table caught my eye. They had not been there when I woke up the first time. I read the card in the flowers, smiled, and put it back. Next to the vase was a note.

Sweetie, Gone to see Mom. Come up to the main house when you wake and we'll have lunch. Forever Yours, Edward

I showered and dressed, not in a rush, but was walking out the door within thirty minutes. As I walked up the path to the main house, I saw Edward and his mother, in the distance walking into the greenhouse. I paused, deciding whether to go into the main house or join them. I chose the house. It had been built during post-Civil War Reconstruction. The original house burnt to the ground only a few short weeks before the end of the war. It was a beautiful brick mansion, not only perfect for parties but for day-to-day living as well.

I found Poppy in the study talking with Victor. I had not heard the conversation, but the two men laughed just before noticing me.

"Well, there she is," Victor said standing. "I think I'll let the two of you talk."

I was puzzled as Victor left the room. I did not know that Poppy had an agenda for me. I kissed him on the cheek and he gestured for me to sit next to him on the sofa.

"What have you done to Edward? That boy is a mess!"

"Excuse me?" I tilted my head. "I have no idea what you're talking about."

Poppy smiled. "Hmm. I think the two of you might be having a communication problem. He thinks you are about to leave him."

"Leave him?" I stood up with every intention of going to look for Edward.

"Cassandra, sit down."

"But Poppy, I need to—"

"I think we should talk first. Sit." I had never defied him and had no intention of starting then so I followed his directions even though I was antsy and anxious to find my husband. "What is wrong? Edward sees it. Vivian sees it. Even I see it. You are not happy, my dear."

"Yes, I know. Vivian has already talked to me about it." I exhaled while bouncing my knee, impatient to go look for Edward. "And as much as I appreciate your concern, respectfully, I think this is something I need to talk to my husband about, not you."

Poppy nodded understandingly and smiled. "You are the sweetest child. I wish all my grandchildren were as considerate as you."

"She is very sweet, isn't she?" Edward stood in the doorway, smiling but it did not reach his eyes which were red and puffy.

I stood and he met me with a big embrace and a kiss on the forehead. I closed my eyes and let time stop while thoughts raced through my head.

I don't know how long we stood there but when our embrace loosened, I looked up at him. "Let's walk out to the tree."

He continued to smile. "I was just thinking the same thing."

The ancient weeping willow was our spot and we often sat under it and talked. As we reached the tree, I realized he planned this trip. An oversized blanket, cushions, a picnic lunch, and champagne all waited for our arrival. I smiled and squeezed his hand in mine. He was really trying to make things better. I took off my shoes and stretched out across the blanket. I thought about the first time we sat here. It was a magical night.

The Harvest Ball was an annual event at Thomas Hall. During the harvest celebration at the winery, known as Crush Weekend, guests are invited to join the family in harvesting grapes, enjoying each other's company, good food and wine, and Saturday night the Harvest Ball formal. Last September's event was my first one in attendance and Edward had taken me out to the willow to watch the fireworks and for a little privacy. We sat, watched the beautiful pyrotechnics, drank champagne, made out, and talked about our lives.

Edward poured us both a glass of champagne and we sat silently as I took a small, polite sip. He opened his mouth to speak but I cut him off as I set down my glass.

"Edward, I need to say something before you say anything. I am not leaving you. If I'm being honest with you, I considered doing just that for a few weeks. But I could never do it. You mean too much to me and I'm not ready to give up on us."

You could hear him exhale as though he had been holding his breath. His shoulders relaxed. He leaned against the trunk of the tree and I leaned back against him. "All I've been able to think about since I woke up is what Henry said about me being one stupid mistake from you leaving and I'm pretty sure I made one last night."

"No, I was being oversensitive. You did the right thing taking her home. I'm sorry. I've been so emotional lately. I don't know what is wrong with me." I rubbed my dry eyes and turned to look at him. Edward pulled me tighter into him and I leaned my head against his chest. His heart pounded like a drum against my ear.

"There's nothing wrong with you, Sweetie. I think we've both been under a lot of strain trying to settle into married life. I promise you though, we'll find our way, together."

Chapter Sixteen

"This weekend went by too fast," Edward commented as we walked hand-in-hand back from having dinner with Vivian and Poppy. The moon shone brightly and the occasional shooting star made its way across the night sky.

"It seems like most of the weekend was Stefanie drama. I'm so over her."

Edward paused, knowing his response would greatly influence my mood for the rest of the evening. As he opened his mouth to speak, his phone rang. He looked at the caller ID. "Let me get this."

My first thought was the same as always when his phone rang. Even when he's not at work, he's at work. We continued to walk through the still, humid air.

"Hey. Really? Yes. That soon? Okay, I'll make arrangements for Tuesday, and we'll sign on Wednesday. Okay. Bye."

"What was that about?" I asked, having no context for the conversation.

"I sold the apartment in D.C. It closes on Wednesday."

I stopped walking, mid-stride although we were only a few steps from our front door. My eyes grew to the size of saucers. I could feel an unexpected flood of emotions welling up inside of me as my eyes began to fill with tears. He had been listening to me. He was serious about putting our marriage back on track and taking responsibility for his part of the derailment. Edward placed his hand on the small of my back and led me through the door.

"What inspired that?" I asked, as I slowly regained my composure.

"A friend of mine from boarding school has been trying to get me to sell it to him for years. It's a good time to sell and I don't need it anymore."

"Are you sure about this?" While I hated the place, he did not.

Edward leaned down and pressed his warm lips against mine. His hands found my hips and gently pulled them into his.

"Yes, as usual, you are right. I haven't been making us a priority and the D.C. apartment was making it too easy not to come home." He leaned his forehead against mine and his voice dropped to a whisper. "I told you that I would fix things. That I could change. Selling the apartment is just another step."

Within seconds, we were leaving a trail of clothes from the front door to our bedroom. His clothes were coming off faster than mine but by the time we dropped ourselves onto the bed, I was only in my bra and panties and he was down to his boxer briefs. His kisses were in a constant state of motion. First my lips, then he created a trail with his soft kisses that skimmed across my shoulder and around to my back. I moaned when he stopped at the nape of my neck, sending an exquisite shiver down my spine.

"You are my everything. You know this, right?"

I shook my head with a small smile. I lost his eyes when I turned my head so that my mouth reached his ear.

"I'm pretty sure I'm not. But I know you love me. And I know you're mine. And that's enough." When I was done whispering in his ear, I was completely bare and so was he.

He exhaled loudly, knowing I was right. He did not try to disagree. Instead, his hands moved softly and firmly along my hips and thighs, working their way up and only stopping when he reached my breasts. He stared at his hands as they caressed my body and then his eyes returned to mine. "My God, you are spectacularly beautiful."

I rolled onto him, thinking I would take control of what was to come next. Before I could make a move, Edward's hands grabbed my hips and lifted me onto him. We quickly found our rhythm, but when I tried to speed up, he flipped us so I was under him and his face was mere inches from mine. He slowed down the pace I tried to set and whispered in my ear, "Not yet."

"Edward," I begged. I had never felt so desperate for him. "Faster."

He slowed even more, his hands skimming my waist and breasts with the lightest touch, knowing it would drive me crazy.

"Not yet," he whispered before gingerly pulling on my ear with his teeth.

This was not the first time he teased me like this in bed. When his strong hands firmly clamped onto my hips, I knew exactly what he was about to do but the sudden change in force and pace left me breathless and drove me just to the edge of being swept away. He lowered his face to mine and when our lips found each other's, it was desperate and passionate. I only remember whispering, "Oh God" before complete ecstasy overtook me.

Afterward, on that Sunday night, as we laid spooned against one another and his arms wrapped around me, for the first time in months I truly believed that things were getting better.

I had not closed the shutters to the bedroom windows the night before and the light pouring in was blinding, making it difficult to locate my phone as the ringing pulled me from my peaceful slumber. Edward had long left for work and I had slept so well I did not hear him moving through the house as he readied himself for the day. After fumbling about, I managed to find my phone and answer it.

"It's Alex. It's happened again." His voice was sharp and anguished. The lingering panic in his speech did not go unnoticed.

"I'm sorry. What's happened again?" I was confused and still waiting for both my body and brain to wake up.

"Cassandra, the vines. Dead vines. How could you forget?"

"No, I didn't forget. I'm sorry. I just woke up."

"It's nine thirty."

"What? Really? I've been so exhausted lately. Give me a few minutes and I'll meet you at 782."

"That's the thing. It's not at 782. It's at 331."

"But Alex," I said as a wave of shock washed over me. "Field location 331 is on the other side of the property."

"I know. Cassandra—"

"If this keeps happening, we aren't going to have any vines left come harvest," I said, interrupting him. I was trying to contain my alarm over the whole situation but knew I was failing.

"If it continues it has the potential to be the demise of Thomas Hall Winery. No vines mean no grapes and no grapes mean no wine. What are we going to do?"

As I listened to Alex, I tried to find a response that would calm his alarmed state. Instead, I could feel the bile work its way up my throat as tears fell from my face. I didn't even hang up the phone. I dropped it on the bed and raced to the bathroom, barely making it in time. I sat, leaned against the cold tile wall, and considered the consequences of ending Thomas Hall Winery. Jobs would be lost and a legacy would be ruined. This was my greatest fear for the winery. I had to figure out a way to stop the poisoning of the vines and get our wine production back on track. I would not allow the winery to close. Not on my watch. It was going to be a long week. And it was only Monday morning.

I threw on shorts and a Thomas Hall t-shirt along with some tennis shoes in order to make my way to 331. I went to grab my work keys out of the bowl on the desk, but they were not there. It was where I always kept my keys. I had separate rings for work and home. My house keys were there but the others were gone. I made a quick sweep of the house but could not find them anywhere. I finally gave up the search and headed out into the fields.

Alex was already there, directing field hands as they started to dig out the dead vines. There were twice as many being removed as were at 782.

"Good God, Alex." I hated to even ask, but it was my job to know. "How much this time?"

"Conservatively, a quarter of a million?"

"Okay. How's whoever is responsible getting onto the property?"

"Sis," Alex began but then paused and shook his head. "No, impossible."

I watched him as he thought through whatever was rattling about in his head.

"What's impossible? Tell me what you're thinking."

"Could this be an inside job?"

It had not even occurred to me. The staff that worked within the gated world of Thomas Hall was extensive but acted like one big family. Main house employees, field hands, production staff, and security all came and went daily. They were extremely loyal and many were second and third-generation employees.

"Who on earth would do such a thing?" Alex asked. No employee had ever sold information or photos to the press. They were all paid well and treated with respect. "If it is an inside job, how were we going to stop this from happening again?"

"I don't know, but it sounds like it's time to call Brian. Again."

Chapter Seventeen

Heads turned when I walked into the Pelican Room at the country club. After the morning's events, I almost canceled this lunch but knew I had to do it sooner or later, so decided to press forward with the day's plan.

I must admit, I looked good. Zoe was not going to let me go into this meeting looking anything less than fabulous. She had chosen a dress from a new collection in her shop and had done my hair, nails, and makeup. The violet short-sleeved dress with a scoop neckline was fitted and exposed enough cleavage to show off my figure but not so tight as to be trashy. My high heels added three inches to my height and gave the illusion of long legs. I added my own jewelry to complete the ensemble. Originally, I had thought to wear the diamond necklace Edward gifted me on our wedding day. Upon reflection though, I decided it was too much for lunch. I sat on the floor in front of the safe on Saturday afternoon, pulling several velvet boxes from it. I decided on a necklace and earring set that Edward had shown up with on Valentine's Day.

It was a pearl necklace where the pearls were separated with tiny, diamond-studded bands.

I was led to a table on the other side of the room. I intentionally arrived ten minutes late in order to insure I would arrive last. I could feel the eyes of the other patrons on me. Several men stared as I moved across the room. I was beginning to realize that Edward was right. Men paid attention to me when I entered a room. I never believed him until that moment. The hum of whispers that began long before I reached the table steadily increased in volume. I immediately second guessed my decision for us to meet in public. The rumor mill was going to have a field day with this meeting, but there was no going back now. I laid my phone, face down, on the table.

"I guess it's safe for me to assume you don't own a watch," Stefanie said snidely.

At first sight, she appeared to be appropriately dressed. She wore a white blouse and a lime green skirt. On closer inspection, it was obvious that the shirt was too big for her and she had tried to make it fit better by tucking it into her skirt. The skirt's waistband was stretched to its maximum size, straining the button that was just above the zipper. The skirt had been well worn and the fabric was showing signs of age at the hem.

I continued to stand as I responded to her attitude-filled remark. "I own a watch. I also own a winery. Some things are of a higher priority than arriving at the country club on time. But you know that. I'm assuming you had nothing pressing since you waited."

After I took a seat and we had placed our drink orders, pineapple juice for me and a beer for her, we stared at one another in silence until our drinks were delivered. The waitress asked about our lunch order and I told her we would need a few minutes.

"I guess I should thank you for meeting me today."

"I have to say I was surprised when your secretary called with the invitation," Stefanie said. "I got the impression you don't like me."

"You got the right impression, I don't."

"So why am I here?"

I was about to tell her when my phone pinged. It was Vivian.

For the love of all that is holy, please tell me I'm not seeing you sitting with Stefanie Hayes at the country club. I'm four tables away.

I flipped the phone back onto the table before discretely looking around until I spotted Vivian with her sisters. My phone immediately buzzed again. This time I didn't look at the message but turned the ringer off.

"I'm hoping you can explain something to me."

"Let me guess, you want my version on what went down with the three of us all those years ago."

"I'd like anyone's version of it."

"The guys haven't told you anything? Sounds about par for the course with them. I'm surprised someone in town hasn't given you all the juicy details." She sounded genuinely shocked that I did not already know the details of this emotionally charged triangle.

"I just know there's a past with the two of them and that my relationship with each of them has started more than a fair share of rumors. Now that I've met you, I understand the gossip was spawned by the fact that we have similar features."

"I've already heard. The minute I got back into town people couldn't wait to tell me every rumor that involved you. Some things never change." She finished off her beer and asked the waitress to bring another. "How much do you want to know?"

"Whatever you're willing to tell me. I figured I'd go to the source before trying to piece rumors together."

The waitress returned with Stefanie's drink and asked to take our order. I chose the Crab Louie and Stefanie ordered the same. She took a long pull on her beer before beginning.

"I guess it wouldn't kill me to tell you. I moved here to live with my grandparents after I graduated from college. Their health was deteriorating, and it made perfect sense since I couldn't keep a job. Getting up in the morning for work wasn't for me. My grandparents owned the old movie theatre in town, so I took over running it. That's how I met Edward. He used to come into the theater with his mother. Vivian loved going to the movies there."

"The Egyptian?" Stefanie nodded. "Edward took me there on our first date."

She continued, choosing not to comment. "So, we started dating and it got real serious, real fast. He practically moved into my apartment next to the theater. About four months in he started talking about marriage. He even bought me a ring."

"Hmm." Edward had told me when we first met that he had never dated anyone he would consider marrying and had never bought an engagement ring. Now, this woman was lying to me. At least I thought she was. I wanted to call her out on it but left it alone.

"Hmm?" She repeated with a snarky tone.

I smiled but my jaw was clenched so tightly that my cheeks were sore. "Go ahead."

"Before I go any further, can I just say these guys have a type," she said. "Apparently that type is anyone that looks like me."

Stephanie was annoying me. Of course, she wanted to make this about her. I really wanted to just slap her and walk out of there. I wrapped my hands around the edge of the seat of my chair, holding myself in place.

Thankfully our food arrived at the table but the waitress lingered filling water glasses. We both took a moment to start our salads. About halfway through, she set her fork down and continued her story. I listened as I ate, trying not to interrupt her. The sooner she told me what I wanted to know, the sooner I could leave.

"Well, about the time I met Edward, I also met Brian. I grew up with guns and loved to shoot. We met at the gun range just outside of town. I would go there to work on my aim at least once a week."

"You were unhappy with Edward?"

"No, it was boredom. Brian was fun and carefree and had no intention of settling down. I guess I wanted to have my cake and eat it too. Edward was always working. He made certain I wanted for nothing and worshipped me but he was never around." This sounded all too familiar to me and I did not like the thought of being treated the same way Edward treated a bitch like Stefanie. I found myself quietly grinding my teeth. "This went on for about seven months and then..."

"And then you got pregnant." I finished her sentence for her. At this point, my phone was vibrating so much it was moving towards the edge of the table. "Excuse me for a moment."

I picked up my phone and there were seventeen text messages from a variety of people and they were all concerning this lunch. My favorites, however, were from Edward and Brian, and they both said the exact same thing.

Have you lost your mind?!

I snorted a quiet laugh and put my phone on the table. "Go on."

"At first, I didn't tell either guy that the baby might not be theirs. It was fun. Edward was excited. Brian was freaking out. It was a real laugh."

I knew my face read of disgust and Stefanie saw it.

"Oh, give me a fucking break. You may appear to be a perfect little princess to the men in this town but most women know better. You can't tell me you haven't loved all the attention this whole scene has gotten you. You know I've heard the rumors. If they're true, you married Edward for his money and are seeing Brian on the side. No judging here, I tried to do the same thing."

"Stefanie, don't ever assume you know me. We are nothing alike. Since you've returned, I've heard about you too. The rumor mill may have gotten you right, but they're wrong about me. I don't double-dip when it comes to men. One's plenty. But you obviously got caught."

"Yeah. The guys didn't know each other then but they were groomsmen in the wedding of a mutual friend. They started talking during the bachelor party. One made a comment about a tattoo I have. They put two and two together and ..."

The smile that disappeared from her face landed on mine. Choosing my words carefully, I only found it necessary to say one. "Busted."

"Things went downhill really quick. When Edward discovered I was seeing Brian too, he immediately broke up with me but told me if he was the father, he'd take care of me and the baby. It wasn't long before I found out there were two babies. The surprising thing was that Brian proposed before we knew whose they were."

"And you accepted?"

"Of course, he wanted me. Even if the twins had been Edward's, he only would have married me for the twins. He wanted to take care of them. Not me, but them. I wasn't going to be placed in order of importance behind two infants."

"You know, Edward's been taking care of them anyway. I don't think anyone knows."

"What do you mean?"

"St. Margaret's. The scholarships. Edward set them up specifically for Gina and Georgie. Everyone thinks they are academic scholarships, and the girls are bright, but the only people who will ever receive those scholarships are your daughters."

"Wow," she said and then sat stunned for a brief moment. I watched as the arrogant mask she wore melted away. "I was wondering where those scholarships magically appeared from. Even after everything he did that for me?"

Just like that Stefanie's mask was back in place, thinking what Edward did was for her and not them.

"He would do anything for those girls. So would I."

"The twins are great, aren't they? They look just like me. I can't believe how grown up they are."

"Speaking of the twins, that was quite the stunt you pulled at the school." She stared at me as if she had no idea that I knew what she had done. "Really? Who do you think picked them up, took them shopping, and had them sleepover so you and Brian could talk?"

"They were at Thomas Hall?"

"They often are or we're at Brian's." This was not a completely true statement, but I wanted to piss her off, and knowing we had time with the girls she did not seem to be doing the trick.

"I guess that means you're responsible for the blue hair too. I hate it. It makes them look less like me." Her reaction made me smile.

"Well, it's not always about you now, is it?"

She made a sour-looking face before she spoke. "Question: How long have you known my girls?"

"I met them not long after I moved to Thomas Hall in September."

"Wait a minute! How long did you and Edward date before you moved there?"

"We didn't. It's complicated." Not only was it complicated but knew it would be ridiculous to try to explain it all to someone so shallow.

"Damn, we were on the verge of marriage and I was never invited to dinner, let alone spend the night."

I did not hesitate when I replied, "Well, the family likes me."

"Even Darla?"

Of course, she would ask about Darla. "She's dead."

"No shit! I always liked her."

"Of course, you did." I should have known. As my dad would say, birds of a feather flock together. We sat in silence for a few minutes, finishing our lunches.

"Stefanie, what happened?" I did not need to elaborate. She knew what I was asking.

"Drugs. That's what happened. I got mixed up with them when the girls were about a year old. That's why Brian split up with me. He told me to get clean or get out.

"Along the way, I got in a situation with my dealer. He told me if I ran some drugs up from Mexico, he'd wipe my debt. On my very first run, I got caught in Arizona with enough cocaine on me to get possession with intent. I tried to call Brian to bail me out, but his mother intercepted my calls and made sure he never knew."

"I take it she wasn't a fan."

"Still isn't. Have you met her?"

"Once, briefly. She doesn't like me either." I paused to have a drink, thinking about my only encounter with Granny Hayes. The twins had spent a few days with Edward and me one weekend in February. Brian was attending a police procedure seminar in Washington D.C. and the girls wanted to spend more time with me. On Sunday evening, Granny Hayes and I finally met face to face. The moment she saw me her facial expression instantly became a mirror to her attitude toward me. Angry and indignant. As fast as she could move, she packed up the girls and their belongings in her car and left without ever speaking. It was only now I understood why. I was a doppelganger to a woman who had crushed her beloved son's heart.

The waitress stopped at our table and asked if I would like more juice. I nodded to the affirmative and asked her to bring the check as well. My glass was not quite empty but within moments a fresh pineapple juice sat in front of me along with the Country Club account slip. The bill was paid monthly, although I wasn't sure if Edward or Vivian were responsible for it.

"So, you've been in jail all this time?" I asked.

"All ten years. It was supposed to be fifteen but thank God for overcrowding, I got out early."

The expression on my face must have betrayed my thoughts. Before I could comment, Stefanie spoke, answering my question.

"Look, I told the girls everything. I figure even if they never forgive me that maybe I can be a cautionary tale. You thought I abandoned the girls, didn't you? I tried to contact them over the years. Is that why you think I'm a bitch?"

"I'm pretty certain I think you're a bitch because you are one." I picked up the pen that the waitress placed next to the check and signed it, not bothering to look at the total. "However, we don't have enough time for me to list all of the reasons why I think you are. And as you can see, I do own more than yoga pants." Stefanie nodded her head once in agreement as I stood to make my departure.

I walked over to her side of the table, bent down until my face was inches from hers, stared into her eyes, and said in a clear tone, "And for the record, I own Edward too. If you ever show up at my house again and proposition my husband, I guarantee you that I have the resources to make your life a living hell for a very, very long time."

I did not wait for a response. I knew those at nearby tables heard what I said and I was glad they did. I turned on my heels and walked toward the exit, head high and standing tall with a smug smirk on my face. I left Stefanie sitting at the table alone, mouth open, and looking shocked. I doubt anyone in the restaurant noticed though because all eyes were on me and for once, I did not mind. As the lunch patrons began loudly whispering once more, I caught Vivian's expression as I glanced when I moved passed her. She was definitely proud.

Chapter Eighteen

I COULD NOT HAVE picked a more beautiful day for a pool party if I tried. It was sunny and warm, but not too hot and, in an unusual occurrence, even for Memorial Day, it was not very humid. A light breeze pushed a few fluffy, white clouds around in the sky and filled the air with the sweet smell of grapes that were just beginning to take shape on the vines across from our home.

It was around eleven-thirty when the staff from the main house began to set up the patio with tables for food, coolers, ice, and drinks. Trays of food were tucked into my refrigerator until they were needed.

I was heading to my room to get dressed when there was a tap on the sliding glass door in the kitchen. "Hello? Cassandra? Are you home?" It was Zoe.

Zoe was possibly the most beautiful woman I had ever met, both inside and out. She always looked perfect for the occasion she was at and today was no exception. Her long legs looked fabulous in the baby doll-length sundress she was wearing as a coverup. After a quick hug, she handed me a small shopping bag.

"What's this?" I asked.

"You mentioned to me you needed a new bathing suit. This just arrived at the shop. It's perfect for you."

I peeked in the bag to discover, in what was my opinion, a ridiculously small bikini. In reality, it was probably one of the more modest ones in her store. There was no way I would ever be comfortable wearing it.

"Uh, no. This is way too small."

"Actually, it's a size bigger than you'd normally wear. We didn't have it in your size, but I think it will work.

Edward, who had been in the living room, made his way into the kitchen. "Can I see?"

I took both pieces out of the bag, dangling them from one hooked finger.

"Looks perfect to me," he said with a Cheshire cat grin plastered on his face. "I can't wait to see you in it."

I rolled my eyes, smiled, and shook my head at my husband's comment.

"You should at least try it on," Zoe insisted.

"Fine," I said, turning and padding off in bare feet to the bedroom.

Five minutes later I was standing in front of the mirror looking at myself in the skimpy red bikini. I never thought I would see the day I would even consider wearing one in public. The top could barely hold my breasts in place and the bottoms felt a bit tight. It was a good thing she did not have it in my size. The next size down would have been too small.

For the majority of my life, I had been overweight and it sky-rocketed after my parents died. Over the years I tried every fad diet on the planet. It wasn't until the death of my first husband that I finally got my weight under control. However, that little plump girl always looked back at me when I stepped in front of a mirror and today was no different.

There was a tap on the door and Zoe walked in, not waiting for an invitation. "Damn girl, you look hot!"

"I feel ridiculous. Do you think it's really okay?"

"It's better than okay. When did you get so busty? Did you get a boob job when I wasn't looking because you definitely fill it out? And you know I would not lie to you."

"Well, if we're being honest could you please tell me why you never mentioned that I look almost identical to Stefanie Hayes?"

"I forgot what she looked like. It's been ten years since I last laid eyes on her. I remembered her having dark hair and fair skin but didn't realize until her recent reappearance how strong the resemblance is between the two of you. The first time I saw her, I thought it was you talking with someone on Main Street until I saw her smoking. That's when I realized it was Stefanie."

"You wouldn't think it would be a big deal but it kind of freaks me out."

"I would imagine so. What's Edward's explanation?"

"He definitely has a type. The two women he's been serious about have similar features. Dark hair, fair skin, and curvy. From what I understand, a lot of the not-so-serious girlfriends looked the same way."

"Now that you mention it," Zoe said while taking a seat in a chair near the fireplace. "He does really have a type, doesn't he?"

I weakly smiled and nodded as I walked over to the closet and found a navy-blue sundress. I put it on over the bathing suit and turned to Zoe as I let out a deep sigh. "The bikini is a bit much. Well, actually, there's not enough of it in my opinion. I'll probably change into my black one-piece later. It has more material to cover me, but I'll leave this on for now."

"Something's wrong, isn't it? You look worried. You don't have to wear the bikini if you're that uncomfortable in it."

"It's not that." I dropped my voice to a whisper. "Zoe, my period is late and this bathing suit is a size bigger than I wear and it barely fits."

"How late?"

"From best I can tell this is the second one I've missed. I've never been predictable though."

"Have you taken a pregnancy test yet?"

"How? If I go into the drugstore in town and buy one, everyone will know before I get home to take the test. I called my OB/GYN in Richmond and made an appointment, but my doctor can't see me until the end of June. She's on maternity leave."

"You are right about the drug store. Does Edward know?"

"No," I thought about how often I had tried to mention it to him lately but could never get the words out. I could feel my lower lip start to quiver and tears filled my eyes. I turned so Zoe would not see. "I'm afraid to tell him until I know for sure. All of the recent drama has made him relive the whole Stefanie pregnancy thing. I don't want him to get his hopes up if I'm not. I think it would break his heart."

As we spoke, I heard *Jimmy Buffett's Margaritaville* through the speakers. I could only guess that guests were beginning to arrive and Edward turned the music on.

Within the hour, almost everyone had arrived. Henry and Zoe arrived first. Zoe never left after bringing me the bikini and Henry was moments behind her. Poppy and Vivian walked over from the main house bringing Victor along for the party, Phoebe and her two children arrived loudly as Noah decided today was the day to torment his sister, and Michael arrived late with his new girlfriend. Karrie was a political lobbyist who was born and raised in Atlanta. She had long, silky blonde hair and a deep tan that intensified the color of her hazel eyes. She was sweet and a little shy. We were almost an hour into the party when Libby-Mae arrived late and looked a little disheveled. Both of these things were highly unusual for her. Alex strolled in a few minutes behind her.

I breathed a sigh of relief when Brian and the girls arrived without Stefanie. I had not invited her but decided if she showed up with them, I would be civil with her for the duration of the party. Gina and Georgie's happiness was more important than my ego.

The twins raced towards the pool and Brian walked over to me. It only took me a split second to realize he was angry. If he had been a cartoon character, steam would have been pouring out of his ears.

"Are you okay?"

"I got into a screaming match with Stef this morning. She wanted the girls for the day, with no notice mind you, and I told her we already had plans. We fought for about ten minutes before I realized the decision didn't belong to either of us. The girls were who it was about. It didn't take them long to decide where they wanted to be. God, Cassandra, every time I think I'm done being angry at her, she finds a new way to piss me off. How am I going to live with her in the girls' lives?"

"I don't have an answer for that one. Sorry." I gave him a quick hug.

"How about an answer for the blue hair?"

"Yeah, I don't have an answer for that either," I said with a grin. "Talk to Zoe."

He shook his head. "I think I need a beer. I am not ready for teenage girls. Especially with Stefanie around."

Once all the guests had been greeted and the heat of the day became unbearable, I decided it was time to get in the pool and then I remembered what I was wearing. Edward swam over to where I sat on the edge, dangling my feet in the water.

"Are you getting in?" He asked, placing a kiss on my left knee.

"I don't think so. I'm still wearing that red bikini Zoe brought me and my body is not bikini ready."

"Your body is always bikini ready. Every curve is perfectly placed," Edward whispered so only I could hear. "Hop in."

I woke that morning feeling bloated and pudgy, but I shyly pulled the sundress over my head and dropped straight into the water in an effort not to be seen.

"God, you look gorgeous in red!" This time he did not whisper, and several people turned to see what Edward was talking about, including Brian, Alex, and Michael. They were having a lighthearted conversation at the end of the pool when Edward drew their attention. I heard the words "Damn, she's hot" blurt out of Alex's mouth. There was no doubt that my face was as crimson as the bikini.

As I felt the warmth fill my face, I heard Edward growl as he squinted at Alex. There was something almost feral about it and I would be lying if I said it wasn't sexy.

While I floated around the pool with Edward, I picked up a couple of grape leaves that had fallen into the pool. After a few minutes more in the water, he grabbed me by the waist, turned me to face him, and planted his lips against mine. It was as if he couldn't wait another moment to touch me. I melted in his arms, savoring the moment when I heard a drunken Brian loudly comment.

"Get a room!"

Edward's lips left mine just long enough to reply. "I've got a room, Brian. Several in fact. Come to think of it, *all* the rooms here are mine."

I giggled just before we finished our kiss and he held me a few minutes longer before I hopped out, grabbed a towel, and wrapped it around my body. I looked around and watched the children playing in the pool, the guys hanging out around the grill talking about baseball, and the older guests reminiscing about their youth. I stood for a moment, took it all in, and smiled.

I grabbed my phone and started snapping photographs of the people in my life that I loved. I wanted to remember this moment because everything was perfect. Unfortunately, this sense of perfect peace always preceded the preverbal rug being pulled out from underneath me. I would not have to wait long for it to happen.

As the party was winding down, I noticed that both Brian and Alex were drunk. I had seen Alex drunk before. He was a happy drunk. He would stumble home at the end of the night and wake in the morning with a headache, vowing never to drink again. However, I had never seen Brian this wasted before. He looked as if everything was triggering him towards anger. While I could not hear everything he was saying to the others near him, it seemed every second or third word was Stefanie.

I was sitting with Poppy and Vivian. He just started telling Vivian about the first time we met, when, on the other side of the pool deck, I heard shouting. I turned to discover it was Brian and Edward.

This was it. The moment I had seen coming for over six months. I was not sure how it began, but I knew it would not end well. I stood to make my way over toward the two men who were just off the pool deck, in the grass, next to the grill. Instantly, Poppy was next to me and put his hand on my shoulder.

"Let me handle this for you." He walked away before I could protest.

"I'm the asshole here? I don't think so. You got what you deserved with Stefanie." Edward's voice carried across the patio, the volume increasing as he spoke as his face became more and more tense. He took a deep breath and I could see him reliving the whole incident in his mind. My heart ached for him. "You have no idea how devastated I was when everything happened with her. It took years to get over it."

Brian smirked. He hit a nerve with Edward and knew it. "This isn't even about Stefanie."

"You're going to regret this when the alcohol wears off," Henry said as he faced Brian.

"Stay out of this, Henry. It's none of your business." Brian then turned his full attention to Edward.

"You can't stand that Cassandra and I are close." He was intentionally prodding my husband into what I was certain would turn into a fight.

"You're right. I hate it. But I trust her, despite her lack of judgment in becoming friends with you. So, whatever makes my beautiful girl happy, she can have."

Poppy stepped between the two of them, hoping to end the argument. "Okay gentlemen, that is enough. Brian, you are drunk. You should let someone drive you home."

Edward ignored the fact Poppy was talking. "But I know you, Brian. You're a son-of-a-bitch. Cassie doesn't see it, but I do. You're going to make a move on her at some point. You can't stand that she's mine!"

The music ended just as Brian smiled and said, "What? You think I haven't already made a move?" That ship has long sailed."

There was dead silence. I knew all eyes were on me and I suddenly felt very naked in the bikini it took most of the afternoon to become comfortable in and looked around for my sundress. I felt as if there was not enough oxygen to inhale even though we were standing outside. I tried to speak but no sounds escaped my mouth.

"Yeah?" Edward asked. Brian had pushed him too far this time snapping the last of Edward's restraint. Before anyone could say a word, I saw the punch coming. Edward planted a right hook into Brian's face, making contact just below his eye. Brian tackled

Edward and both men hit the ground but my husband continued to pummel my best friend. At some point, Brian's nose began to bleed and I felt myself sway at the sight of it.

My stomach churned and I wondered if I would be able to avoid being ill. Something had to be done about these two men. This had to stop. I only knew of two ways to keep this event from unfolding. At least one was illegal and involved firearms. Michael and Henry managed to separate the two men before I decided what to do. Brian's nose looked broken and his eye was beginning to swell. He broke free of Michael's grasp and managed to punch Edward in the abs before Poppy's voice bellowed.

"Enough! This has gone too far. You have upset Cassandra and that I will not allow." Tears began to slide down my face as my own anger over their childish behavior intensified.

"You are both acting like teenagers," Poppy said, lecturing them. "I do not know what the deal is with the two of you and your obsession with having the same woman. You both need to figure it out for her sake."

I watched as Poppy looked around to insure no children were within earshot. "And so help me God, if I find myself addressing this with either of you again, I will have a couple of my associates personally show you how much this infuriates me. And I cannot guarantee you will not be breathing through a straw when they are done with you!" I heard Brian mutter the word "damn" and Edward lowered his voice to a more respectable volume before saying, "okay". A statement like that, from a man like Poppy, was not a threat, but a promise. A promise you did not want him to act upon. It took a moment for me to comprehend that he had just threatened, not only to physically destroy my husband but a member of law enforcement as well. This was spiraling out of control.

"Thank you, Poppy," I said as calmly as possible after walking over to join him. "I think I should take it from here."

I turned my attention to Brian. "Just because I declined your advances doesn't mean you have the right to use it as ammunition. I'd think you'd be a little more civil to Edward. If for no other reason than he pays the tuition for both girls to go to Saint Margaret's."

"No, he doesn't!" He sneered. "They are there on a merit scholarship."

"You mean you don't know? I was sure Stefanie would tell you after our lunch. Who do you think funds those scholarships? And why they were started to begin with? That's how much Edward cared for Stefanie. He wanted to make certain her girls got a good education. Whether they were his or not." I paused, exhaling before continuing. I looked at Edward who was surprised I knew all of this even though some of what I was saying was mere speculation. I never confronted after learning he on paid the girls' tuition and he had no idea I was aware of it. When I glanced back to Brian, his drunken expression had me asking questions I did not know to ask until then. Step by step I slowly moved in his direction while I spoke.

"Did you make that move on me because I was Edward's? Because I looked like a carbon copy of Stefanie? Did you really even want me for who I am and not who I look like?" I knew everyone had noticed the resemblance by now, so I felt no shame whatsoever in mentioning it. "You know what? Don't answer that. It doesn't matter."

I turned toward Edward, who was looking at Brian with a condescending smile plastered across his face. "And you! Wipe that look off your face. I haven't even begun to address your schoolyard behavior!" He did as he was told and swallowed hard.

I took a moment to collect my thoughts and as I did, I watched Zoe whisper in Henry's ear. The two gathered their things, tapped Alex and Libby-Mae on the shoulders, and they all began the short walk back to Henry's house. Phoebe gathered her children and followed her brother.

"We will see to the twins," Poppy said as Vivian and Victor collected their things and headed into our house. The girls had hidden in the house out of embarrassment. I didn't blame them. I wished I could have followed their lead. I waited until they walked across the field, heading to the main house, and Michael and his date made their way to his car before I said anything more.

It was just Edward, Brian, and me. I planted the two men in patio chairs and sat between them. I said nothing for a minute or two trying to figure out what direction to move the conversation. Once I opened my mouth to speak though, the words began to just fall out on their own.

"What the hell is wrong with the two of you?!" They had only ever heard me swear once or twice and their eyes widened with my question.

"I want some answers and I want them now. This," I said pointing back and forth between the two of them, "This has to stop immediately. I have neither the time nor energy for this nonsense. You know what? On second thought, I don't want answers. I want a solution."

I loudly exhaled before continuing. "Whatever issues the two of you have began long before I arrived, at least fourteen years ago. And to be honest, I don't care. But hear this, I refuse to choose one of you over the other. As a matter of fact, it shouldn't even be a choice. One of you is my spouse and the other is my friend. The two of you should be able to at least exist civilly when at the same events.

"What happened today is completely unacceptable. Edward, the fact you could not control your temper over something trivial is childish! And you, Brian, whatever made you think this was the time or place for that discussion is completely ludicrous. My private life is just that, private. The fact that people know that you tried to stop Edward and me from marrying by making your move is incredibly embarrassing to me. You knew my wishes and intentionally ignored them!"

I could feel tears begin to well up again and blinked them back. I was so emotional as of late. I just could not keep my feelings in check anymore. Edward, recognizing my distress, slid his chair closer to mine and softly wrapped a single arm around my shoulders. I sat in the moment, eyes closed, trying to compose myself and decide what to do about these two men. As I did, a few tears escaped from my eyes. I could not fix this and I knew it. They had to do it themselves.

Standing, I kissed Edward on the forehead before walking past Brian pausing to pat his shoulder. It was then I noticed that Brian was beginning to sober up. Henry was right, he would hate himself in the morning. He would probably hate himself sooner than that. What I said next shocked me nearly as much as it shocked them.

"The two of you are going to stay here until you work this out," I said, eerily calm. "I don't care if you talk, scream, laugh, or even pulverize each other. But when the two of you leave this patio tonight, this will be resolved, permanently. Once you're done, call up to the main house and someone will drive Brian and the girls home. He's too wasted to drive."

As I moved toward the door, Edward caught up to me, causing me to pause. "You're not staying?"

"No. I don't need to see this. You just need to fix it." I leaned into him, momentarily burying my head in his chest before continuing into the house.

As I did, I heard Brian say to Edward with a truly remorseful tone, "What the hell have I done? I've never brought her to tears before."

To which Edward replied, "Gut-wrenching to know you're responsible for that, isn't it? Okay, Brian, this ends now. We won't be putting Cassandra through this ever again."

Chapter Nineteen

TUESDAY MORNING FOUND ME walking into the police station with a coffee of the day for Brian and an iced chai latte for myself. Rain the night before had caused the humidity to skyrocket. How Brian could drink something hot in this weather was beyond me.

I paused at the front desk and the clerk waved me through. I was a regular enough fixture at the station where the clerks no longer asked to state my business or whom I wanted to see. I made my way to Brian's office where I found him sitting with his elbows propped up on the desk, holding his head with his hands. He only looked up after I sat and slid the coffee under his nose.

"Mmm, coffee. Thanks," he said looking up but not looking at me. The purple crescent under Brian's eye and his bandaged nose remained as evidence of the Saturday evening brawl. "After the other night, I don't really know what to say. I guess an apology is the best place to start. I really am sorry for my behavior."

"I know. You've been under an enormous amount of stress recently. It was just unfortunate for me that you chose that moment to excise your frustration." We sat in silence for a few minutes. It was only when he finished his coffee did he continue.

"I imagine Edward told you about our conversation, before and after the fight."

"Actually, no. He offered but I don't really care as long as you two resolved things."

"I think we did. We both agreed to be civil toward one another."

"Good," I hesitated to continue.

"But…?" He said, sensing I had more to say.

"I need to ask you something. And I just need you to be honest. Okay?" Brian nodded his head. "I know I said I didn't care about the answer to this, but I think I do. It's been gnawing away at me since the party, actually longer than that. Was your interest in me because of my resemblance to Stefanie, an attempt of some nature to hurt Edward, or because you liked me?"

"You know, the first time I saw you when you were at the movies with Edward, I was certain Stefanie was back in town."

"You're avoiding the question."

Brian turned his head and looked out the window. "You're probably my closest friend, Cassandra."

"That doesn't provide me with any answers. When we first met and became friends, what was your intention?" I paused, reflecting on a more recent theory of mine, and then continued asking questions. "Brian, was your interest in me because you thought I would make a good mother for the girls? If you think the resemblance between the girls and me has gone unnoticed in town, you're highly mistaken."

"What would you say if I said I was looking for a new and improved Stefanie to help raise the girls?"

"A version of Stefanie? I'd be highly insulted."

"Well, that wasn't the case." I was not certain he was being honest.

"What was it then?"

The silence in his small office was like a vice. It was then I knew, he wasn't going to tell me. When I stood to leave, he stopped me.

"Cassandra, I don't think you completely understand the history I have with your husband." He still could not look me in the eye. It told me all I needed to know. His initial actions had not been honest and possibly not even caring. I thought I was prepared to accept any answer but I was wrong. My heart ached to think the person I called my best friend would even consider using me so selfishly. And as I walked out of the police station and onto the street, I wondered how long it would be before I stepped foot in there again.

In an unusual occurrence, I found myself at the main house at lunchtime. I sat in the dining room with Poppy and Vivian discussing everyone's plans for the remainder of the week. When Poppy discussed his return to Chicago that afternoon, I had an idea.

"Poppy, would you mind if I flew to Chicago with you? I need to get away. I'll only stay a couple of days. I'd like to do some shopping, maybe take in a show. I think a change of scenery may be just what I need."

He thought about it for a minute, which surprised me. Previously, he had always enjoyed my company. It seemed like an eternity before he spoke. "Cassandra dear, you are always welcome to travel with me, but are you certain this is the proper time for you to be heading out of town? I need to leave in the next half hour."

"I can pack in ten minutes and I think getting away is exactly what I need."

"You better hop to it then," Vivian said before Poppy could further comment. "I've got to stay here for a couple of things on my schedule. This will be wonderful. I hate it when Poppy has to travel alone." I looked at his expression which was more serious than I had seen in a long time and I felt like a rock had dropped into my stomach.

I walked over to my house to pack and as I did, I let my thoughts form freely. Maybe a short getaway would give me time to put the whole pool party fight in perspective. I had nothing pressing on my schedule. While I threw clothes in a small suitcase, I called Libby-Mae and informed her of my change in plans for the rest of the week. I had two meetings that were easy to reschedule and Libby-Mae told me she would inform Henry and Alex of my whereabouts.

Four hours later, Poppy and I landed at Chicago's O'Hare Airport. Within minutes we were seated in the back of his limo and he was on the phone. Poppy was basically commuting back to Chicago for work the same way Edward did working in Washington D.C. However, in the last few months, I had seen much more of Poppy than I had of my husband. That seemed to be changing though.

I pulled out my phone and sent Edward a text.

Decided to go with Poppy to Chicago for a few days. Going to do some shopping and put the pool party in perspective. Plan on coming home late Thursday. In Chicago now and my phone is on.

About an hour later, my phone rang. It was Edward.

"Hey, Honey," I answered on the first ring.

"See, *this* is the way to run away from home." I did not need to see his face to know he was smiling. His voice told me everything I needed to know. "I know where you are, that you're safe, and in good company."

"You don't mind?" I was initially worried about Edward's reaction when I decided to do this so spontaneously.

"No, I really don't." I was not one hundred percent convinced he was being honest. I spent a great deal of time questioning my husband's honesty over the last couple of months. I truly had not forgiven him for Bermuda yet. "But Sweetie, when did you decide to do this?"

"About thirty minutes before Poppy left for the airport."

"Sounds like the good old days for you." It seemed the family dinner had opened Edward's eyes to some of the sacrifices I made when I married him. We never discussed the points made about everything I gave up and I did not know if he had absorbed that information.

"A little. I always forget how much I like Chicago until I come back. If nothing else, the shopping is fantastic. Your American Express card may not survive the trip though." Rarely did I shop, but there were some clothes I was in desperate need of. Some shoes too.

I heard Edward chuckle. "Hey Sweetie, do me a favor and stop in that lingerie shop I like and pick out something new to wear when you get home. I want to unwrap you like a present."

"That's all you want to do?" I asked, trying to be flirty. Just as I finished my question, I could hear people coming into Edward's office in the background.

"I've got to go, but before I hang up, the answer is no. I'll call you tonight and elaborate."

I giggled.

I was settling into one of Poppy's luxurious guest suites when, with my back to the door, I heard someone walk in without bothering to knock. I was always placed in the same suite when I visited Poppy. It was the closest suite to the library and had a cream and mint color palette. The canopy bed and lace curtains always made me feel like a Disney princess. It was the type of living quarters every little girl would love to have. My late husband hated it, but Poppy was insistent that we always use the room because I loved it so much. It was the first time since Tony's death that I had stepped foot inside Poppy's house, let alone this suite. I never knew why, but it always smelled like strawberries and when I inhaled the air in the suite, a rush of memories, both good and bad, flooded my mind. When the person cleared their throat, I snapped back to the present.

I turned toward the door to discover Tony's sister. She didn't speak but came at me at full speed, only stopping when we were inches apart. "What are you doing in my house, murderer?" The last word was said with tightly clenched teeth. Izzy had wasted no time terrifying me with both her words and presence. I had two options, stand still in terror or try to talk my way out of it. I decided to do both.

"First," I tried to say politely while still frozen in place, "the last time I checked, this is Poppy's home and he invited me to stay. Second, and more importantly, I did not kill your brother. Even though he went to great lengths in an attempt to destroy me."

"Destroy? You haven't seen destruction yet. But you will. Poppy may think you're a sweetheart, but I know there's a stuck-up little bitch in there! You killed my brother and you're going to have to answer for that!"

I knew who had murdered Tony, and I thanked God each and every day that person had done so. When I was finally brave enough, I stepped back, trying to create space between the two of us. However, she took a step every time I did, giving me no more room. Just when I realized I was running out of space and would soon be trapped in a corner, Poppy appeared in the doorway.

"Isabella Martin, leave Cassandra alone. Now! She did not kill Tony and you know it."

"Poppy," she began. "I know—"

"Child, you know nothing. We talked about this before. You will not treat my guests in this manner. One more time and you will not be welcome in my home. Now go!"

Izzy did an about-face and walked out of the bedroom, only slowing when she turned sideways to get past Poppy and averting her eyes as she did so. She knew she had crossed a line with Poppy and that was something you just did not do. Had she been stupid enough to look up, she would have seen a scowl that only a mob don could deliver. It scared me a little and it was not even directed toward me. When I heard the sound of her heels hitting hardwood, I knew she was at the end of the hallway. Poppy and I listened as the sound moved further and further away.

Poppy shook his head, exhaled a deep breath, and a kindhearted expression returned to his face. "I am so sorry, my dear."

"Is my being here going to cause a problem? I can always check into a hotel. I don't want to be the reason for any trouble."

"Absolutely not! You are staying right here and that young lady is going to be dealt with immediately. I am not done with her yet. I came by to let you know that an associate of mine dropped off two tickets for the theatre on Thursday night. Would you like them? I have been to the theatre with Vivian more in the last six months than I have in my entire life. They are for a musical called Hamilton."

"Hamilton?! Do you know how hard it is to get tickets to that show? Edward and I saw it on our honeymoon when we stopped off in Puerto Rico. I think the tickets ended up costing close to a thousand dollars each."

"Is it really that good?"

"Yes! And I would happily see it again." He handed me the tickets. Front row, center seats. "Poppy, you should go with me. It's different from anything you've ever seen. And it's about an immigrant making it big in the early days of America's history."

"I had not planned on it but let me see if I can move some things around on my schedule. I think going to the theatre with you would make for a very enjoyable evening. Vivian, the beautiful woman, always wants to know the whole story and listen to the soundtrack multiple times before going to a show. I would never say so to her, but I prefer to let it unfold on stage and be surprised."

Chapter Twenty

The library at the Scarpelli mansion remained unchanged from the first time I entered it, many years ago. Mahogany bookcases lined the walls. It was obvious they were custom made as specifically sized openings held statues, framed photographs, and a large black safe. The room had floor-length windows on the east side of the room. The heavy maroon velvet curtains were closed to the light leaving the room in total darkness. I fumbled along the wall next to the door, until I found a switch. Upon flipping it, the room filled with a soft, peaceful light. Bright enough to read by, but not harsh like the florescence in my office. I made a mental note to myself to look into having the lights changed out in the production building at Thomas Hall. This lighting would be much more pleasant for work.

I skimmed the bookshelves until I found a book that piqued my interest and made my way to one of the two brown leather sofas near the fireplace. There was no fire lit today, as the weather was past cold days and nights, even in Chicago. I opened the book and began reading about the history of organized crime. I am uncertain how long I sat reading before I heard footsteps behind me.

"I think you are the only person who has ever actually used this room as a library," I smiled, closed the book, and turned to give Poppy my full attention. I was mildly surprised to find he was not alone. I gently placed the book on the side table and stood, smoothing the forest green wrap dress I was wearing.

"Cassandra, I would like for you to meet my associate, Mr. Gino Mantegna. Mr. Mantegna was a tall man who towered over Poppy with broad shoulders and muscular arms that only a bespoke suit could hold. We shook hands and exchanged pleasantries and when we were done, I turned to Poppy.

"I'll leave you and let you conduct your business." Before I could take a single step, Poppy stopped me. "Mr. Mantegna will only be here a moment. Stay." Poppy walked over to his desk. It was mahogany, identical to the shelves, with locks on each drawer. He sat as they spoke. The men kept their voices low, but I heard words like extortion and planned hits. I did not try to make excuses or justify to myself what Poppy said. I knew what he did was unlawful and unethical but it was not the first time I overheard Poppy having a discussion like this. For him, it was just another day at the office. I watched as he unlocked one drawer, retrieved a manila envelope, and handed it to the gentleman.

"I'll call you when the job is finished," Mr. Mantegna said as he glanced at me, obviously concerned about what I had just witnessed. Poppy noticed too and smiled.

"Gino, you have nothing to worry about. She is family. She understands."

Poppy was right. I did understand. I did not necessarily agree with the path his life had taken but I respected his decisions. And we were family.

The gentleman smiled and once said his goodbyes and left, Poppy hit a button on his desk and a butler appeared.

"Bring the young lady and me a bottle of Pinot and something to nibble on." The butler left and I waited until Poppy sat on the sofa before taking a seat across from him. "I want to talk to you about something that has been on my mind lately."

In all honesty, I was too tired for conversation. I spent the morning at the Field Museum which had the Dead Sea Scrolls on special exhibition, followed by lunch at Park Grill near The Bean sculpture. That in itself would have been a full day. However, I chose to walk "The Magnificent Mile" after lunch and spend some of my husband's hard-earned money.

Since I was a guest in Poppy's home, I would never deny him conversation. No one ever denied him anything. It was never a chore for me to spend time with Poppy though.

"What's tonight's topic?" This question was always how we started evening conversations. I am not certain when or how it became the norm, but it was our thing and we always raced to see who could say it first. On this occasion, I won.

He smiled as he pointed to the book I had been reading. "Organized crime."

"That's a new topic for us."

"Exactly. You have never asked me about my business. Ever. Why is that my dear?"

Before I could answer, the butler returned, placing plates, napkins, two glasses, a bottle of wine, and a charcuterie tray on a nearby table. A second tray followed a moment later, delivered by a young man with chocolates, petit fours, and ginger snaps elegantly arranged.

We took a moment and fixed plates for ourselves while the young man poured the wine. Once the staff left, closing the door behind them, I took a moment to savor a taste of the wine and was pleasantly surprised. I looked up at Poppy, who was already smiling.

"This is one of ours," I said, setting my glass on a table. "But it's not from the case I sent you."

"Heavens no. That case was gone by the beginning of February. And four more since. I made the mistake of serving it at a dinner meeting with my consiglieres and now every time they are here, they ask for your Pinot Noir."

"You should have said something sooner. I'll have a few more cases shipped in the morning."

"Cassandra, my dear, you are always so thoughtful."

I paused, debating on whether to return to the original topic of the evening. Before I could speak, Poppy brought the conversation back to the beginning.

"So, what would you like to know about the organization?"

"If you don't mind me asking, what makes you think I want to know anything about it at all? As you said, I've never asked you about your work." I watched Poppy's eyes drop to my hand where it rested on the book next to me that I pulled from the shelves earlier in the evening.

"You have not. At least, not directly. But I have suspected that lately you would like to know more. And tonight, your reading material has given you away."

I smiled, looking at Poppy just long enough to make his face light up and form a grin while watching my expression.

"You're close but slightly off target. I'm more curious about your life and how *you* ended up the head of your organization. Not so much the business itself. I've always had the feeling that the less I know about the family business, the fewer lawyers I'll have to hire someday."

Poppy chuckled. "You are probably right about the lawyers, but certainly you have heard about my rise to the top of this business. Tony shared that with you, did he not?"

"No, sir. Tony rarely told me anything." A sudden silence cloaked the room. I could not speculate what Poppy's thoughts were, but I felt the same way I felt whenever I thought about Tony. A deep sense of both loss and relief. "All I know is that you immigrated to the United States in your early teens and lived with your aunt and cousin."

"Well, my dear, that is as good of a place to begin as anywhere else. I was actually only ten when I came to the United States from Italy in the late fifties. The SS Goethalis. It was a long trip. Especially for the Third Class passengers. I promised myself then that someday I would only travel First Class."

I smiled before asking my next question. "Who did you travel with on the journey?"

"No one. My mother saved for two years just for my ticket. The idea was that I would go first, live with my aunt, and make money to send home to Italy so the rest of the family could come as well."

"How long did that take?"

Poppy's face gleamed with pride. "I had all twelve here within five years."

"Is that why you..." I did not know exactly how to ask the question so I let my voice drift away and left the question hanging. It did not take long for him to realize this and continued.

"I, for lack of a better description, fell into the business. My cousin, who was three years older than me, was an errand boy for a group of soldiers in the Marazoni family. I started following him around and before long I was an errand boy for a different group of soldiers in the same family. I was well-liked and moved up the chain at a quick pace. Let me stop here for a moment. Do you know the hierarchy of an organization like mine?"

"Not really. I know there's a boss, you, and there are soldiers at the bottom of the pyramid, besides that, I'm clueless."

"Well, it sounds like you have the basic idea. It is a slightly distorted pyramid. Actually, let me do this." Poppy walked over to his desk, found a piece of paper and a pen, before spending a few minutes writing rapidly and drawing lines. When he returned to his seat he handed me, for lack of a better term, a family tree. But this was one like no other. It included names and phone numbers, not many, but names, nevertheless. "Here is how my organization looks."

"Poppy, you should probably shred this paper," I said, setting it back on the table. "Names? Isn't that dangerous?"

"Cassandra, I did it for a reason. Hold on to that paper. If something happens and you cannot reach me, these are the people you should contact for assistance."

"Why wouldn't I be able to reach you?" I felt the same pit that formed in my stomach the day we left for Chicago. "You always take my calls."

"You have been part of this family for a long time. I think you know the answer to that question." And he was right. I knew the answer, I just didn't want to admit it.

"Is something going on that makes you think your days are numbered? Is that why you hesitated before agreeing to let me come with you to Chicago?" I was asking a lot of questions tonight on a subject I had always avoided.

"Yes, that is why I hesitated. It is just a feeling I have had lately. It may be nothing but paranoia, but I was concerned I might put you in danger. Honestly, I still am."

"You didn't say anything because you didn't want Vivian to worry."

"Exactly." Poppy paused for a moment. "I have convinced Vivian that we should take a trip to Italy next week. It will keep her out of Chicago and safe."

I watched as a bittersweet expression crossed his face. I knew it was meant for both Vivian and me. He seemed to silently convey that he would miss us when he met his end. I felt there was something more he wanted to say to me. I tilted my head slightly upward and looked him in his eyes. "Poppy, say what you need to say."

He smiled and said, "You have grown into such a wonderful woman. There is beauty in your strength. Never forget that." Then his voice dropped in both volume and pitch. "Take care of Vivian if—"

I raised my hand, gesturing for him to stop. "Of course. Please tell me you are being careful though. I couldn't imagine a world without you in it." My eyes filled with tears and I blinked hard to keep them from falling. However, a few made their way down my face and I tried to wipe them away.

Poppy moved from the other sofa to sit next to me and lifted my hand which lay on the sofa and clasped it in his, lifting it, and kissing the back of my hand. When I looked at him, his tender eyes left me feeling like he was saying his goodbyes and my heart ached at the thought of a world without Poppy. He took a handkerchief from his pocket and used it to pat the tears dry from my face. "Cassandra, my sweet child. I have had a long and happy life. Men in my position tend to die young and not from natural causes. I am old, but I do not think natural causes will be my demise either."

Chapter Twenty-One

Thursday afternoon, two dresses were draped across the bed. I could not decide which one to wear to the theatre. My attention was distracted by the ringing of my cell phone.

"Hi, Gina. Hi, Georgie. What's new?" Whenever the twins called me, they always had me on speakerphone.

"No, it's just me, Gina." Worry oozed from her voice. I could envision her in her room with the door closed, stretched out across the bed. There was no doubt in my mind that she and her sister had argued about something and her face was still red with anger.

"What's wrong?"

"Georgie's in a panic. She thinks you're mad at us. I told her that wasn't true, but she won't listen. She thinks all the women in our world are mad at us. You, Granny, Mom."

"Okay, first, I'm not mad at y'all. Your dad and I had a little falling out on Tuesday and I'm in Chicago right now with Mr. Poppy." They had only met him at the party but were as fascinated with him as he was with the two of them. The three sat for over an hour, discussing food, music, and all the sites to see in Chicago. "I'll be back tonight and will probably see your dad at the first of the week. I can never stay mad at my friends for long. And I never meant to alienate the two of you. It's only been five days since the pool party. I think maybe she's being a little dramatic, don't you?"

"You're right. She's such a drama queen. I just don't know what to do about her." I could almost hear Gina's eyes roll and it made me smile.

"As for your Granny, why is she mad?"

"Well, I'm not a hundred percent sure but I think she's mad because we've been spending time with Mom and she really seems to hate her."

"I'm not sure your grandmother really likes anybody. However, I do know that she doesn't like me, so I'm probably the wrong person to ask for help with her. But tell me, what's going on with your mom?"

"I don't know. She said she'd come get us last night for pizza, but never showed up. When we called the house she's staying at, the lady she rents a room from said she left Tuesday afternoon and took all her stuff with her. No one has seen her since. Aunt Cassie, what did we do so wrong that she's left us again?" Gina sniffled. Although she would never admit it, Gina felt betrayed by her mother. My heart broke for them both. The next time I saw that woman it was not going to be pretty.

"Gina, honey, you've done nothing wrong. There is obviously something broken in her and it isn't your job to fix it. But when I get back, I promise I'll help you find her."

And Stefanie was going to wish I hadn't.

The drizzle that fell all day finally stopped sometime during the show. Poppy and I took our time leaving the theatre, carefully crossing the street, so as not to slip on the wet pavement. Stilettos were not the best choice for footwear that evening as they held no traction.

Poppy upped his security detail for the evening. Usually, it was a driver and one large guard. Leaving the play, there were four guards in addition to the driver.

"I liked it. Honestly, I did." Poppy said as he turned to face me. "I was not certain I would like Hamilton, but it surprised me. He led quite a life. Thank you for suggesting I join you." I smiled as he spoke of the evening, both of us genuinely happy.

That's when I heard it. At first, I thought it was a champagne cork popping from a bottle and it startled me. But it wasn't. Everything unfolded so quickly that there was nothing anyone could have done to stop it.

The guards behind us dropped to the street, like discarded marionettes, followed by the two in front of us. I felt an intense, blistering pain in my left arm. I turned to face Poppy in time to see blood and brains spray around us and Poppy's lifeless body collapse onto the cement. I did not realize I was heading to the ground with Poppy's body tumbling over mine until I felt the smack of wet asphalt against my head. The driver, seeing what was transpiring, opened the car door and raced towards Poppy, only to collapse onto the closest guard.

The next time I opened my eyes, I was in the ambulance. The burning in my arm remained and I asked the medic if my grandfather was in a different ambulance, but he didn't answer. I remembered that he had been shot and realized I had too. I turned my head to see my arm wrapped in bandages that had fresh blood seeping through. The sight of the blood made me nauseous and I tried hard not to faint again. However, moments later, my vision went blurry and everything went dark.

The bullet had gone out of its way to only graze my arm, doing minimal damage and while I had a headache, I did not have a concussion. I did need stitches both on my head and arm though. I was waiting for my discharge papers in the emergency room when my cell phone rang.

"Thank God you decided not to go to the theatre!" It was Edward and I heard him breathe a sigh of relief. "I've been losing my mind for the last ten minutes. I was afraid to call you out of fear you were dead and then the first time I tried it went straight to voicemail."

"You heard already?" I asked.

"I just saw a special news report. It said Poppy and his guards were gunned down outside a theatre in Chicago earlier this evening," he said, taking a deep breath and blowing it out before continuing. "I knew you said the two of you were going to see Hamilton and the report said that everyone in Poppy's entourage died."

I sighed; completely aware it was audible. "Yeah, about that. I did go. I was with him. I was the sole survivor."

There was a long pause before he said anything and when he did speak, the volume was reduced to a whisper. "How many times am I going to almost lose you? Are you okay?" I could hear the panic in Edward's voice rise and fall. "Why did they say everyone died?"

"I'm fine. There was a concern that the shooter might try to finish the job if they knew I was alive. So, the cops told the press everyone died. Edward, it was a professional hitman. It was too planned, too precise to be anything else."

"I don't feel like you're safe now. If the shooter was a pro, he'll try to finish the job." He had not heard me say the same thing moments earlier. He was in a dazed state of shock. I could hear it in his voice. I wished I were home with him, spooned together under the blankets of our oversized bed.

"Honey, I just said that. Poppy's people have guards all over the emergency room. I'm fine."

"You keep saying you're fine but you are in a hospital. That's not where people go when they're fine, Cassandra." Edward's voice sounded louder and more panicked with each word than it had before.

"I know. I hit my head on the pavement and the paramedics wanted me to be checked out by an ER doctor. My original plan was to take a late flight to Richmond, but I missed the flight because of Poppy's death. I'll be home in the morning. And really, I'm fine." I decided the fact I was grazed by a bullet and had stitches could wait until we were face to face.

"Fly to D.C. instead. You keep saying you're fine but I need to lay eyes on you, Sweetie. This has really freaked me out. I almost lost you." His voice cracked as he spoke. "I can't believe I almost lost you again."

"Honey, I'm fine. What's sad is that I'm not freaked out at all. I feel like this is typical for my life."

Chapter Twenty-Two

I STEPPED OFF THE plane a little before ten the next morning. I was searching for a Chesapeake Biotech driver when I saw Edward. He was unshaven and had dark crescents under his eyes. He looked nearly as exhausted as I felt. There was no doubt in my mind that he never went to sleep and paced the floor this morning until it was time to go to the airport.

When my eyes found his, I breathed a sigh of relief and a layer of tension left my body. Within seconds I was wrapped in his arms. I heard him loudly exhale as if he had been holding his breath since last night. He pulled me away from him and I watched as he scanned my body looking for bruises, cuts, and bandages. I knew he would do this again later once we were home and I was wearing less clothing. I would tell him about the bullet grazing my arm then. When he was done Edward guided me to the limo while the driver handled my luggage.

"Cassie, Sweetie, I hate this, but I've got to go back to the office for a while. I want you to come with me."

I nodded my head in agreement before wrapping my arms around him and burying my face in his chest. From the moment the plane landed this was all I wanted so I completely ignored my phone blowing up. I was certain I would have a hundred text messages by the time I bothered to look at it. But I did not care.

Neither of us spoke as we made the short trip into the heart of the city. We just held each other. I was so happy to be in his arms. I always knew that home was where the people you loved were, and I was definitely home.

I had only been to Edward's office a few times since we met. Chesapeake Biotech occupied the top three floors of a building with stunning views of the Capitol, Mall, and Washington Monument. When the elevator opened, the voices of those in the office lowered to a quiet hush. The staff always turned my presence into an event.

I was glad I had taken a few extra minutes to blow out my hair and apply a light layer of makeup. I was wearing a gray pencil skirt and a white blouse, its long sleeves concealing my bandage-wrapped stitches. I removed the large bandage on my head after I showered at the hotel replacing it with a small flesh-colored Band-aid. I left my hair down and it covered the bandage almost completely.

Edward guided me through a maze of desks and cubicles leading me towards his office. He had a tight grip on my waist and kept me pulled close to him. As my high-heeled shoes clicked across the floor I saw Edward's assistant, standing at her desk. Kelly waited for me to reach her before giving me a hug.

"I am so sorry, Mrs. Baker." Normally she would call me Cassandra, but whenever I was in the office, she would address me more formally. She did the same with Edward.

"Thank you." I was acutely aware of how exhausted I sounded.

"Sweetie, let's go sit in my office." His voice was comforting and I felt more of the tension in my neck and shoulders dissipate every time he spoke.

I turned and walked into his office and he closed the door behind us. As soon as the door shut, I pulled myself tighter into him. Tears immediately began to drip down my face. It was the first time I had cried about Poppy's death. Until that moment I had been acting on autopilot.

I never went to sleep after the shooting. Instead, I gave the police a detailed statement and how to reach me if they needed more information. Then I collected my things from Poppy's home, as quickly and stealthily as possible, doing my best to avoid the multitude of people who had descended on the house. It was impossible to avoid everyone, but most people steered clear of me. One of the family's bodyguards had been instructed by Mr. Mantegna to assist me in avoiding Izzy, escort me to the airport, and guard me until I boarded my flight.

I arrived at the airport around two in the morning. After arranging a ticket for later in the morning, I checked into the Hilton in the terminal. I stripped out of the blood-splattered clothes I was still in and took the longest shower of my life, tossed the clothes I had previously removed, and ate room service. By the time I had done these things, it was time to get ready for my seven o'clock flight.

Edward guided me to the sofa against the wall of his office and we sat. He looked at me no doubt wondering how far into despair I would let myself fall. On two separate occasions, I suffered from nervous breakdowns when under extreme stress. He witnessed the last one and it scared him. He knew I was sleep-deprived and stressed. Edward tried not to let it show, but the worry showed on his face. I continued to cry for a few more minutes before letting the tears subside. When I was done, he gently brushed his lips across the Band-aid on my temple before handing me a handkerchief out of his jacket pocket and I used it to dry my face.

"Thank you," I whispered as I leaned into him, letting him wrap his arms around me. We sat enjoying the silence until Kelly's voice came through the intercom.

"Mr. Baker, I'm sorry to interrupt but your eleven-thirty appointment is here. Should I reschedule it?"

"Yes, please."

I spoke up before she could disconnect. "No. He'll take the meeting. Give him five minutes."

He leaned his head around to look at me. "Sweetie, are you sure? Because you're not going anywhere until we talk about this. I have a lot of questions for you."

"It's okay. I'm thirsty. I'll go get something to drink and harass Kelly for a bit. Get your work done, Honey." I gently pressed my lips against his before I walked out the door.

Kelly walked a trio of businessmen into the office and quickly returned.

"Mr. Baker told me not to let you out of my sight. He's worried."

"He has just cause, but I'm going to be fine," I said. "What's Edward's schedule like for the rest of the day?"

"It was full, but I'm rescheduling some things. He'll be free until two thirty after this meeting. I'm going to try to clear the day. I think the two of you need it." Kelly looked around. Several dozen people were milling about, doing their jobs. "Let's go down to the lobby and get something to drink from the coffee shop. Fewer ears to hear things and start rumors."

As we rode the elevator down, my arm began to throb. Since pain pills were currently not an option, I reached into my purse, retrieved two Tylenol, and swallowed them, not bothering with water.

Kelly noticed and as we exited the elevator she said, "Are you okay? Nothing personal but I've seen you look better."

"Last night was a bit much. I don't think I've processed it all yet." I hesitated, debating how much I wanted to disclose concerning a recent discovery. I decided I needed to talk to Edward first. "I haven't slept since the night before the shooting either."

"And the Tylenol?"

"I sustained some minor injuries last night." I put my fingers gently on my temple. "I'm fine but my head is throbbing a little. That reminds me, can your wife take some stitches out next week? You could come for dinner." Kelly's wife, Margie, was a physician. While I did not know her as well as I knew Kelly, I always enjoyed her company and used any excuse I could find to get the two of them to Thomas Hall.

"I'm sure she would be happy to make a house call. You know she loves the new chef at the main house. If she were to leave me for a man, it would be him." Kelly and I laughed and then paused so we could place our orders. Once we were seated at a bistro table with our iced teas, she continued the conversation. "If I'm prying, tell me to shove off, but are the two of you all right?"

"You're not prying. You are one of my dearest friends." While we hadn't known each other long, she really was my closest girlfriend aside from Zoe these days. "I hardly know. I mean, for a couple of months, we were never together. I thought things were getting better, but then last weekend..."

"Ah, the pool party. I heard about that. And a killer red bikini too! Your husband has mentioned it several times."

"I'm glad you were out of town and didn't see the fight." I ignored the bikini remark but was certain my face was flushed from embarrassment. "Kelly, I thought I knew what we were getting into when we got married. I really thought I could live in Edward's world. I just didn't think I'd be so lonely when we weren't together. And for a while, we were hardly sleeping in the same house, let alone the same bed. I was beginning to wonder why we bothered getting married at all. I've lived alone before and it was never a problem. Why is this so different?"

"It was never a problem before because you didn't have another option. Now that you have Edward, you know what you're missing when he's not around."

That was it. That was the difference. While it seemed obvious, it was the difference I had not been able to pinpoint.

I was not aware that Edward was standing behind me until he leaned down and kissed the nape of my neck. Kelly, unbeknownst to me, had texted him when we headed to the elevator. I smiled and he whispered in my ear, "So you miss me. That's what this is really all about?"

As he spoke his hand slid from my shoulder onto my arm. He lifted his hand quickly and I turned to see what caused him to do so. The palm of his hand was red. Fresh blood. Not a lot, but just enough to absorb through my shirt sleeve and alarm Edward when the palm of his hand came back bloody.

"Cassie, you're bleeding. We need to get you a fresh bandage."

The edges of my vision began to turn dark and I blinked hard in order to remain conscious as Edward steadied me with both hands. Blood was one of the few things that could make me faint and Edward had witnessed this enough times to know I could easily fall out of the chair in which I was seated. It was then I realized that fainting was probably how I survived being gunned down with Poppy. It must have been mistaken for death by the shooter.

"Sweetie, I think it's time for you to tell me exactly what the hell happened in Chicago."

By the time evening rush hour began in D.C. Edward and I were home at Thomas Hall laying across the bed. I had been waiting all week for Edward to ask a certain question and it finally escaped his mouth. "You never told me that Brian made a move on you. What did he do?"

"He kissed me." Edward's eyes said it all. He did not like the idea of another man's lips on mine.

"Why didn't you tell me?"

"Because it didn't mean anything to me." The night he kissed me it had meant something but I soon realized it only provided solace at a vulnerable moment when I was furious with Edward.

"I don't think that's true, Sweetie. Everything means something to you. It's one of the many things I love about you. I think the reason you didn't say anything is because he's your friend and you didn't want me to beat him up."

"It appears I failed on that front."

"When did it happen?"

"The night I kicked you out of the house in November." I knew he wanted me to elaborate but I was determined to say as little as possible on the subject.

"Son-of-a-bitch," He murmured as he shook his head. "I knew leaving him there alone with you was a mistake. What else did the two of you do?"

"Nothing. I think the question you really want to ask is did we sleep together? Which, with the history the two of you have, I kind of get, but I'm not happy with the insinuation. You know me better than that."

Edward ran his fingers through his hair and then wrapped his arms around me. "I'm sorry. You're right. I'm not really sure what I was asking. God Cassie! I was never the jealous type before I met you. Now I don't even like it when other men look at you."

"Then maybe you shouldn't have been so excited about the bikini Zoe brought me."

He gave me a small smile. "Yeah, but I liked seeing you in it so sacrifices had to be made."

I laughed and shook my head before continuing. "Brian gave me other options besides marrying you, that's all. I couldn't even consider them though."

"Why?"

"Because I'm not in love with him. I never have been. I only love you." Edward pulled me close to him and his warm, wet lips quickly found mine.

It did not take me long to ask the question he had to know was coming. "What exactly was your relationship with Stefanie? And don't give me that 'it's a small town' explanation. I didn't believe you the first time you said it, so I won't this time either."

"Okay," he said with a sigh. "We met at the Egyptian Theater. It must be over fourteen years ago now. I was in my thirties. Her grandparents owned it and Stefanie was managing it. We started dating and I thought she was the one."

"She was the one serious relationship you had in your thirties?"

"Yep, I had no idea she was seeing Brian on the side. When she told me she was pregnant I was over the moon excited. It was only when Brian and I discovered we were both sleeping with her did she tell me that she didn't know if I was the father."

"Edward, are you? Are Georgie and Gina yours?"

"I wanted them to be, but they aren't mine. They belong to Brian and Stefanie. I was devastated when I found out. I think it was at that moment I resigned myself that there was no one out there for me and decided to just pour myself into my work." Edward's serious face suddenly became bright and happy as he pulled me tighter into his arms. "And then I met you. Looking back, I really dodged a bullet with her, didn't I?"

I nodded in agreement. "And it never occurred to you to mention that we look almost identical?"

"But you don't."

"Edward? Really?" I am certain my voice was suspicious sounding.

"Look, I know I have a type, but in my eyes, you are very different from her." As he spoke, he rolled my stockings down my legs, one by one, tossing them across the room. "Your eyes, besides being a different color, are bigger and rounder. And even though your mouth is smaller, your lips are fuller and more irresistible. When you laugh you get these cute dimples on your cheeks. Her face doesn't do that. Your boobs are so much better than hers. Do I need to go on? Because I haven't even started to comment on your sweet little ass yet?"

"Okay, okay." I knew exactly what he thought of my butt because he told me on several occasions.

"That's a reasonable answer, I guess. Shut up and kiss me," I said and after what began as a long, slow, wet kiss I found his lips moving along my neck. They did not stop there though. Edward's mouth kept moving until he formed a path down my body and between my breasts before giving each one the attention he felt they deserved. He had pulled another magic trick and removed all my clothes when I was distracted by his lips. He was still fully dressed when he continued his trail of kisses, occasionally nibbling or sucking on my skin as he made his way past my belly button and continued down me until I begged for him inside me. Even exhausted, I loved every minute of his attention and how much he seemed to enjoy himself as well.

Afterward, we lounged in silence, enjoying each other's company. I was staring at a painting across the room, trying to figure out how to tell him something. Something big. It was then I realized Edward was talking but I wasn't listening.

"I'm sorry. My mind wandered off somewhere else. What did you say?"

Edward laughed. "You really don't like that piece of art, do you?"

"Calling it art is a bit of a stretch. How did you end up with it anyway?"

"I'm not exactly sure. I think the decorator picked it out. We can change it out for anything you like, Sweetie." Edward grinned. "What do you want to do tonight?"

I knew what my husband was up to. After I told Edward about the shooting we ordered in lunch. While we ate in his office, we had a conversation that he felt needed to be had. He was adamant that I needed to be more selfish and tell him what I wanted, needed, liked, didn't like, and most importantly what did and did not make me happy. He spoke all the way through lunch. I never got more than two words at a time into the conversation. I wasn't sure I completely agreed with him but decided I would try it for a few days and see how it felt.

"Tonight, I want to eat pizza in bed, fall asleep in your arms while watching a movie, and then wake up in the morning and make love again. What do you think? Is that okay with you?" My big news could wait one more day.

"That, my dear, is a fantastic idea."

And that's exactly what we did. Well, sort of. The next morning, I found myself in the bathroom, leaning over the toilet, regurgitating last night's dinner.

I rarely remembered my dreams, but every nightmare I remembered as though it were engraved in my brain. I woke several times that night in a cold sweat, having relived the last few minutes of Poppy's life on a continuous loop. Edward held me tight through each nightmare, hoping to comfort me. Needless to say, the next morning I was too exhausted to make love to my husband. And he was sleep-deprived. Instead, we spent a wonderful day snuggled up together in bed.

I did not feel up to being around others or eating in the dining room of the main house, but nevertheless when it was time for Sunday dinner Edward and I found ourselves walking into the foyer of his mother's home. The walk had been hot and sweaty as humidity filled the early evening air. When we came through the door, we were blasted by the air-conditioning and the scent of the lasagna that would be the main course.

Everyone was there, including Libby-Mae and Zoe. This was surprising to me as I understood that Sunday dinner was family only, with no exceptions. There was only one Sunday after we met before Edward and I were engaged. And there was no Sunday dinner that night because Senior was dead and I was in the hospital.

We were barely through the door before Vivian's arms were tightly wrapped around me.

"My dear, I am so sorry," she whispered in my ear as she held me. It was then Poppy's death truly shook me. I had been in shock and later wept, but this was different. The feeling left me hollowed out. When I spoke, I did not recognize my own whispering voice.

"Vivian, I feel horrible for you."

"You knew him much longer than I did. I am just happy Poppy and I had the time we did together. We knew we wouldn't have long. Neither of us were young when we met."

Edward tucked me under his arm and pulled me close as I mumbled, "You should have had longer." I was tired. I should not have been. Edward and I spent the entire previous day in bed, but it seemed to have not been enough.

I knew the night would be hard to manage and I was right. One by one, each person made a point to come to me and offer condolences. When they inquired about my well-being, tears welled in my eyes and I whispered the words, "I'm fine."

The main course had just been served when a wave of exhaustion poured over me and I wavered in my chair, swaying as though I might fall out of it. This did not go unnoticed by my husband. Without saying a word, he lifted me out of my chair and carried me out of the room, up the stairs, and into his childhood suite.

As we moved away from the dining room, I heard Henry ask, "Mom, I was just thinking about everything she's endured since arriving in Virginia. How much more do you think Cassandra can take before it all completely breaks her?"

"Son, she's stronger than you think. Right now, she's just doing what she needs to in order to get through this."

Their voices faded as we moved away from the dining room and mere moments later Edward was placing me on his bed and I was instantly asleep, wrapped in his arms. We would not leave the room until the sun came up. That is when we headed home to get ready for the day before Edward headed to Washington, D.C.

Chapter Twenty-Three

It was definitely a Monday morning. I walked into my office, already feeling like death warmed over, only to find Alex and Henry drinking coffee. It was only eight o'clock but the tension in the room told me whatever was happening was going to be an all-day thing. I walked over to my desk and sat a few files I had taken home on it. When I did, I noticed that Libby-Mae had made a new set of work keys for me and put them on a keychain with a small silver disk with Thomas Hall's logo engraved on it. I did not know such a thing existed.

When I looked up at the guys, I saw previously unseen stress weighing upon them.

"Why do I have the feeling I should have crawled back into bed?" I had considered doing so when we returned to our house but convinced myself it was a bad idea and took a long, hot shower before heading to work instead.

"You are going to wish you had, Sis," Henry commented as he fixed himself another cup of coffee.

I looked at Alex and read his face like a book. The vines had been attacked again.

"Damn it all!" I yelled at the top of my lungs and I slid most of the items on my desk onto the floor with one swipe of my arm. Both guys turned to look at me with mouths and eyes open wide. After regaining my composure, I asked, "How bad is it this time?"

"Double," Alex said, the heartbreak seeping from his voice.

"Double the last time?" I asked, looking for clarification.

"No. Double everything that has already been destroyed."

I sunk into my office chair and exhaled heavily. I sat pensively as the sounds of the warehouse made their way into my office in whispering tones. Regardless of the plan I was trying to formulate, I knew this situation would not end well.

"I'm going to make some calls, but I think we need to have all the shareholders in for a meeting. Here. Today. Henry, can you call Vivian? Call Phoebe too."

"Cassandra, Phoebe's not a shareholder."

"Neither is Edward, but they're both family. I'm going to try to get him here as well. Maybe Kelly can move some things around." Edward had relinquished his shares of the winery to me not long after the first of the year following an epic argument about the future of Thomas Hall Winery. He felt, and I agreed, it would be better for Thomas Hall, and our marriage, if our shares were managed by one person. By doing so, he pushed me into an interesting position. Between Edward's shares, the shares bought from Phoebe, and the shares willed to me by Senior, I was now the majority shareholder. I controlled fifty-five percent of the winery. While I no longer needed anyone's permission at all to do anything at the winery, I would never make any major decision without the family's approval. "I think we're on the verge of shutting down. This may be the end of the winery."

After several phone calls, it was decided the shareholders' meeting would be held over dinner at the main house. Everyone sat at the dinner table. I included Edward, Phoebe, Michael, and Libby-Mae in the invitation to the meeting. They weren't shareholders but this directly impacted them as well. Michael arrived just as the first course was being served, carrying stacks of folders. He placed them on a side table and joined us as well. Once the meal was over and any evidence of it had been cleared, I was ready to start the meeting. I had taken the seat at the head of the table, at Vivian's insistence, and sat thinking about the winery. Somehow, despite my desire not to let it happen, the winery was on the verge of collapse. I spent the entire day examining the most recent attack on the vines, talking with our security team, and crunching numbers over the phone with Michael. None of these things yielded positive results.

I let out an audible sigh before I spoke. "Okay, let's get this over with. As you know we've had multiple attacks on the fields. Someone is trying to sabotage us. We can't figure out who or why. Security, which is now managed by Brick and Bubba, can't figure out how whoever is doing this is getting inside the gate and onto the property. Alex and I agree that it may be an inside job. But here's the thing, regardless of who is doing this, it's about to bankrupt us." I paused and rubbed my temples with my fingers. As I did, Michael passed out the files he brought along with pens.

"It can't really be that bad, can it?" Phoebe asked.

"Cassandra swore, screamed, and pushed everything off her desk this morning. Including a laptop," Henry commented.

"Oh shit," Phoebe murmured under her breath.

"The last time she did any of those things in unison," Edward said, trying to lighten the mood, "I got kicked out of my own house." Everyone chuckled quietly and I just smiled and shook my head.

"Okay, back to business. We have now conservatively lost over seven hundred thousand dollars in vines, lost revenue, and replacement costs."

"Actually, that number is not correct," Michael interrupted. "That was just a rough estimate. The correct numbers are in the written report."

I flipped open the financial report in the file that he had handed out, along with everyone else. I skimmed through until I found the bottom-line amount. It was $1.2 million. I grabbed the edge of the table for support as I stood, absolutely stunned. "Christ! Michael, are you sure this is right?"

When I looked up, every person in the room could see the anguish on my face and made no comment about my tone or language. Michael nodded his head. I had never known him to be wrong with numbers and he was always ready to defend or explain the financials, but he knew I wasn't ready for that tonight. I remained standing as I looked through part of the paperwork before I continued. "In addition to all of this, today I discovered that the winery is extremely under-insured. Even with the insurance payout, we will have to spend enough money in clean up and replacement that we will no longer be able to make the payroll come January first. And that's assuming the executives, meaning Henry, Alex, and myself, don't take a paycheck. I'm fine without, but I think the guys are going to need to get paid."

Alex interrupted. "I can make do with half pay."

"Same," Henry added.

I looked at Michael, who was steadily tapping away on the calculator app in his phone. After waiting for what seemed like an eternity, he finally looked up and said, "October twenty-fifth will be the last day you can make the payroll then."

"I know each of you is thinking I could have done this over the phone, but I wanted everyone here in person to brainstorm. We need ideas. Somehow, someway to survive this. Now, can someone please come up with something." After a long pause, I casually said, "I'll be right back. I have to go throw up my dinner now."

I heard quiet laughter as they thought I was joking. When I turned to walk away, and sped up my pace, the laughter stopped.

Edward followed me into the library and knocked on the powder room door as I flushed the toilet. "Are you okay in there?"

"Just give me a minute. I need to peel myself up off the floor."

The door to the bathroom opened. Edward looked at me and sat down on the other side of the threshold. "How long has this been going on?"

"I've been sick a lot lately. I'm pretty sure it is stress-related." I was lying. I knew exactly why I was sick, but I was not ready to tell him. I was not ready to tell anyone yet. The whole idea sent me into a spiraling panic. "It seems like if it's not one thing, it's another."

I tried to smile at my husband, who looked concerned, thoughtful, and then I could almost see a light bulb go on over his head as he had a revelation. Only then did he smile back. This was the moment I should have told him, but I did not. I was not ready to say it because that would make it real.

"Feeling better?"

"I think so," I stood up and then quickly crouched back over heaving the remainder of my stomach's contents into the toilet. When I was finished, I looked up at him and said, "Now I'm done. Let's get back to the meeting."

We sat at the dining room table debating ideas when Libby-Mae looked at me. "I have an idea," she whispered. "I know it's not a permanent fix, but it might get us through the rest of the year." I could tell she was intimidated by the company she was in, and I did not blame her. She was nineteen and fresh out of high school.

"Talk to me," I said, trying to keep her focus on me as we always spoke freely to one another.

"We need to liquidate all of the inventory. I'm not exactly sure how yet though. Maybe some event here at the winery? There's over half a million dollars in that cellar. Probably closer to a million."

"That's actually a good idea. Sales seem to be a strong point for you. You've been doing the job of a sales director for the last three months. Unfortunately, I can't give you a raise right now. Take the empty office next to Henry's and we'll use it to devise a plan to make it happen. Remember though, you won't be doing this alone. It's all hands on deck and everyone will be available to assist. We're going to have to think out of the box if we are going to survive this crisis."

"One thing," Edward said. I could not bear one more thing, but he continued to speak before I could interrupt him. "I'll be paying for Crush Weekend and the Harvest Ball out of my own pocket this year. It will continue to happen."

"Thank you, Honey," was all I could say as I looked at him leaned back in his chair, legs stretched out, jacket off, tie loose, and the top two buttons on his shirt undone. God, he was sexy.

We returned to our house around eight and before nine, Edward was dozing off on the sofa. I convinced him we should go to bed early, as he would not go without me. By nine, he was snoring and I was wide awake. He had been more exhausted than usual lately and I blamed it on the daily commute. I could not have been more wrong.

Chapter Twenty-Four

Somehow, I always knew this day would come. The day I dreaded, but it came too soon. No twenty-seven-year-old newlywed expects it to happen to them. But then again, I was no normal newlywed either.

Alex and I were walking through the fields, examining the vines. It was early June in Virginia, and the temperature was already a sweltering eighty-five degrees at ten in the morning. The humidity had the two of us covered head to toe in sweat and the summer sun beat down on us as Alex taught me how to decide where and when to thin the fruit on the vines. I loved days like today. I was outdoors in the sun and heat and Alex was teaching me something new. In other words, I was in heaven.

Libby-Mae jumped out of a golf cart on the path before it came to a complete stop. She ran down the row of vines and stopped in front of me, handing me my cell phone. I left it on the charger on my desk.

"It's Kelly," she said. "It's urgent." She leaned over, breathless from her mad dash and eyes watering over. Alex leaned over and the two began to speak.

"Hey, Kelly. What's up?"

"You need to come to D.C.," There was a pregnant pause. "Something's happened to Edward."

"What?" As I spoke, I found Alex and Libby-Mae walking with me toward the golf cart.

"I'm not sure. It all happened so fast. He was complaining of pain. Then the paramedic was there. Then we were in an ambulance, then the hospital. They just wheeled him into surgery." I heard her sob quietly into the phone.

I felt my chest tighten and my breath shallow and quicken. Somehow, the golf cart was pulling up to my house. I had no idea how we got there. Alex was driving, but I did not remember the golf cart ever moving.

"What was the pain, Kelly?" She didn't respond. "Kelly!" I snapped her name again, hoping for a reply. "I need you to hold it together just a little longer."

"Cassandra, the helicopter is on its way to Thomas Hall. It will bring you and Vivian to MedStar Washington Hospital." I knew she was on autopilot at this point. Whatever happened must have been traumatic. Kelly was always calm. It was her nature. In the nine months since we met, I had never known her to be shaken like this.

As we walked into the house, I grabbed a small carry-on bag from the coat closet by the door. Libby-Mae started packing the black leather briefcase Henry gave me for Christmas. Alex made himself useful by pouring the three of us glasses of iced tea.

"What was the pain, Kelly? I need to know."

"I called Henry. He went to tell Vivian. She'll meet you at the helipad. Henry sounded like he was coming up too."

At this point, I had packed enough casual clothes to get me through a couple of days and pulled a pale green short-sleeved, above the knee dress from my closet, along with sandals, underwear, and jewelry and laid it all on the bed. I went back to the closet and grabbed the matching cardigan. Hospitals were cold places.

"Kelly, what is it you don't want to tell me?"

"It's his heart," she finally blurted out. The minute she said it, I felt my own heart drop into my stomach. Over the last six months, I had seen all the signs. Edward had dismissed his high heart rate to any number of factors and I hadn't pushed him to go to the doctor. A wave of guilt flooded my thoughts. It was a wave I would drown in for years to come.

Libby-Mae walked into the bedroom to see if she could help. I handed her the phone and moved from a first gear crawl into fifth gear, autobahn speed. Within a second, I was naked and in the shower. I washed my hair and scrubbed the sweat and grime from the fields off my body. In less than twenty minutes, I was dressed, make-up and jewelry on, my still wet hair pulled up in a bun with a single clip and I was walking out the door with purse in hand. Alex followed behind with my briefcase and carry-on.

"Libby-Mae, cancel everything you can for the next week and reschedule. Anything urgent, pass to Alex. Except the wine show in Richmond next weekend. Take it over for me."

"Me? Are you sure? I mean, I just graduated from high school."

"Yes, I'm sure. You've done eighty percent of the work for it anyway. Call the printer and have some business cards made. The title on the cards should read Sales and Marketing Coordinator. If you find the job overwhelming, we'll move you to something else later, but you've been doing the job for a while now already. You've been overdue for a promotion and raise since about a week after you started working for me. If we survive the current winery crisis you will be getting a big raise. Get someone from the production room to go with you that knows how these wines taste. I know you're starting to get a feel for it, but I'd rather not advertise that our nineteen-year-old employee knows what our wines taste like. You're still a couple of years away from legally being able to drink."

Alex spoke up. "I'll go with her. Between the two of us, we'll have it covered."

"Great," I said and then turned back to Libby-Mae. "Can you work full-time instead of part-time starting today?"

"Yes, Ma'am."

We were standing at the helipad and I could see Vivian and Henry walking from the main house. I looked up into the sky through my favorite pair of sunglasses but didn't see the helicopter yet.

"Alex, you're in charge. I'll call Michael and give you the ability to sign invoices. If it's a major expense though, call me."

"Of course."

Henry and Vivian were next to us now. I knew I would be okay as long as I didn't look at Henry. Outside of my husband, Henry and I were the closest of the Bakers. I loved him as much as I had loved my own brother. I knew if I made eye contact with him, I would fall apart.

Vivian walked over and silently reached for my hand, squeezing it tightly. I looked at her, dressed perfectly, every hair in place, looking cool as a cucumber. I took a deep breath and exhaled as the helicopter came into view.

When we arrived at the hospital Kelly was waiting for us. Wordlessly, she guided us through corridors toward his room. Vivian and Henry entered the Cardiac ICU with Kelly. Just as I reached the door, a nurse in her late fifties approached me and introduced herself as the charge nurse for the floor.

"Miss Baker, we need some information to complete Mr. Baker's records. We still need his family history." She handed me a clipboard as she spoke. "Mr. Baker's secretary took care of the rest." I knew she meant Kelly, even though she was so much more than just a secretary.

I silently stared at the form. *Does the patient have a family history of (check all that apply):* followed by an extensive list of ailments. I did not know. How could I not know? Edward and I had never discussed our medical histories. The nurse seemed to realize my state of shock and tried to console me. However, what she said only made things worse.

"Don't worry about it. We'll have your mom handle this as soon as we see her. Your father is going to be fine."

I narrowed my eyes, clenched my teeth, and silently counted to ten so I could gain my composure. "My mother-in-law is probably a better source for that information. She's in my husband's room now."

While the nurse looked embarrassed, I didn't wait for an apology. I turned and walked into Edward's room.

I was not prepared for what I saw when I entered the Cardiac ICU. I was so anxious to confirm that Edward was alive that I forgot what I was walking into and it stopped me in my tracks. I almost didn't recognize the man in the bed as my husband and blinked hard while staring to confirm it was indeed him. His lips seemed thin with age while his skin was nearly gray and the lines around his eyes looked deeply etched into his face. When did this happen? When had he aged so much? I saw him every day now but did not realize how many more silver strands had crept into his hair. In my eyes, he was always a tall, broad-shouldered, strong man. Now, somehow, he suddenly appeared to be small and frail.

Looking around the room, I was almost afraid to approach him. He was attached to so many machines that constantly beeped and made bizarre electronic sounds. There was no peace to be had in the cold, sterile, fluorescent-lit room. How Edward was ever supposed to recover in this setting, I had no clue.

A doctor entered the room and headed in my direction when Vivian cleared her throat and directed the man to her instead. I breathed a sigh of relief as I took a seat next to Edward and placed his hand in mine.

"Do not disturb his wife right now. She just arrived and needs to be with her husband."

"But ma'am, legally she's his next of kin."

"Doctor," I said, not even turning toward him but continuing to stare at my husband. "I give you permission to talk with either of them for the duration of Edward's hospital stay."

He turned to speak to Vivian and Henry. I didn't want to even try to listen. Lifting Edward's hand, I kissed the back of it and held it close to my heart.

After the doctor finished briefing Vivian and Henry on Edward's condition, he came over and stood beside me. "Mrs. Baker, I've given your family a full breakdown of everything that happened. I just want you to know the following, your husband is going to be fine. He's actually in good shape now. He won't have to stay long."

The doctor turned to leave when I stopped him. "How long until he wakes up?"

"About half an hour."

"Thank you, for everything."

The doctor reached into his pocket, retrieving a business card. "If you need anything, here's how to reach me."

The next thirty minutes were possibly the longest of my life. As I sat with him, my mind raced, configuring a hundred different *what if* scenarios.

What if he dies?

What if he never wakes up?

What if he has another heart attack?

But the last ones broke me.

What if I never get to tell Edward about the baby?

What if this baby never gets to meet his father?

At some point tears started running down my face, but I did nothing to stop them or wipe them away. I kept thinking this had to be a nightmare and I would wake up in my own bed with Edward, spooned up against my back, playing with my hair.

I stood and leaned over the handrail of the bed, putting my ear to his chest with my watery eyes facing away from his head. His heart sounded, well, normal. It sounded like it did the first time I leaned against him, which while relatively recent, seemed like a lifetime ago. And then, in what was a miracle to me, a shaky hand pulled the clip from the back of my head and wove its fingers into the pile of hair that had been released.

"Mmm. My raven-haired angel," Edward said hoarsely. I shut out everything and everyone around me the moment I heard his voice. I turned my head to face him and he stared at my tear-stained cheeks. "Oh, Sweetie, don't cry. It's going to be okay."

"This is my fault. If I had just—"

"No, it's not," he said, his voice still no more than a whisper. I nodded my head and he gave his a small shake. "I just had heart surgery and you're going to argue with me?"

"I guess not. I'm sorry, Honey."

"I'm not. I just realized that I'm going to be able to get you to agree to anything for a while if I just tack 'I just had heart surgery' onto the end of the request." A classic Edward smirk appeared on his face.

I had no clue how to respond to him. I wanted to laugh at his remark but I was certain the terror I felt was obvious in my expression. I opened my mouth to speak, but no words made their way out. I just gazed into his beautiful brown eyes and silently thanked God that Edward was alive.

Time froze and I had no clue how long we stayed in that position. Me, listening to his heart, him, playing with my hair, and the two of us staring into each other's eyes. However, neither of us had moved when my still smiling husband drifted off into unconsciousness.

I did not leave the hospital the first night. Henry, Vivian, and I sat for hours as Edward slept, waking occasionally, and asking for water to quench his thirst. At some point, Vivian left to make accommodation arrangements for us. It would have been simpler if Edward had not sold the apartment, but the hotel across the street had a three-bedroom suite that was nice and convenient. Even if he still had the apartment, I would have opted for the hotel. Henry left about an hour later when Vivian texted us the room number and mobile key information.

Sleep only came to me in short fifteen to twenty-minute naps in the recliner next to the bed. Technically, I wasn't supposed to be in the ICU, but the nurses said nothing.

A little after three-thirty in the morning, the lead nurse for the night came in and sat next to me. She was tall and thin, with long brown hair pulled into a ponytail, and wearing purple scrubs.

"Can I get you anything?" She had a gentle voice. "Coffee?"

"No, thank you."

"You haven't eaten or drunk anything all night. How about a bottle of water? The other nurses are starting to worry about you."

"I guess I could drink some water."

The nurse left and swiftly returned with a bottle of water and a clear plastic box containing grapes, cheese, and crackers. "I thought you might like this too."

I took the snack and drink from her. I gulped half the bottle before setting the food and water on the nightstand. "Thank you."

"Anytime you need anything, all you have to do is ask."

"I don't want to take you away from your patients. I just appreciate you letting me stay."

"This is his first heart attack, isn't it?" I nodded, fearing that I would start to cry if I spoke. "Have you two been married long?"

"No, not even a year. I just thought, I just thought we would have more time before... This wasn't so supposed to happen so soon. I need him better; he has to get better." I reached down, placing my hand on my stomach and my eyes filled with tears.

"You're pregnant?"

"He doesn't know yet. I just found out a few days ago."

"When was the last time you left that chair?"

"I don't know. I'm sure it's been hours."

"You need to move around a little. Go for a quick walk while Mr. Baker is sleeping."

"No, what if something happens and I'm not here?"

Just then, there was a knock on the door. A short, round woman with ebony skin, short hair, and pink scrubs walked in. "I'm here to take some blood."

I looked at the nurse. "Maybe I will go for a short walk. Blood makes me queasy."

"Just knock on the door to the ICU when you're ready to come back in and I'll come open it for you."

I nodded my head, abandoning my snack and turning the corner to head out the door. The lights in the ICU were dim, but when I opened the door, the fluorescent lights in the hall momentarily blinded me. As I paused, letting my eyes adjust, I heard the two ladies in my husband's room speak.

"Daughter?"

"Wife."

"She's beautiful. Very young too. Gold-digger?"

"No. She hasn't left his side since she got here. We didn't have the heart to kick her out when visiting hours ended. She just sits next to him and holds his hand. So devoted. It's not fake either. I was talking to her when you came in. She's honestly afraid of losing him." It was the first time a stranger had said something positive about me when discussing the age gap between us. It gave me hope that the gold-digging accusations would not last forever.

Once my eyes adjusted, I wandered down the hall, thinking I might go to the cafeteria and get some hot tea. But when I looked at my watch, it was three fifty-five in the morning. They wouldn't be open yet. I continued to walk until I came across the hospital chapel. I eased myself into the first pew and stared at the altar. It was very non-denominational, very sterile, much like the rest of the hospital.

"I know you haven't seen as much of me at church lately, God, but I've got to ask you, is all of this really necessary? I know you're supposed to have a master plan for everything, but this is just too much. I can handle when stuff happens to me. I mean, I'm not too fond of it when people try to kill me, but I can endure it. But Poppy and now Edward? It's too much."

I reflected on my life and relationship with my maker. When my parents died, I turned to God for solace. When my brother killed himself, I turned to Him for acceptance. When I thought my first husband was dead, I thanked God for mercy. When Poppy died, I did not turn to God. I knew the nature of his business was something I would never be able to mesh together with my religious beliefs and I had made my peace with that.

I could not wrap my head around Edward's heart attack though. "Why do you hurt the people I love? What have I done to deserve this? I just want to be loved. Is that really so wrong?"

I closed my eyes and listened for answers from God, but none ever came. Only another question. How could God allow one person to lose so much and still demand more from them?

I sat for a while longer, praying for a sign, but one never came. So, I stood up, walked out of the chapel, and made my way back to Edward. When I was once again seated next to him, I ate the grapes brought to me earlier and then held his hand until Vivian returned at sunrise. Only then did I leave when she ordered me to go to the hotel to shower and rest.

Chapter Twenty-Five

Two afternoons later, I walked into the hospital room after grabbing lunch in the cafeteria, only to find Edward on the phone. He was beginning to look more like himself. The color of his skin was evidence that his health was improving. Unlike the day he was admitted, his skin was a healthy shade of flesh-tone pink. He seemed stronger and looked larger than life once again. It was then I realized that God had been listening, I just needed to trust His timing. In the hospital chapel, I wanted immediate answers and that's not the way it works.

I could tell by the tone of Edward's voice that he was on a business call. When he was working, he used a harsher, sharper voice than when he spoke to me. I watched him for a moment before the spark of aggravation I initially felt about this rapidly grew until my frustration hit a boiling point and I snapped. I yanked the cell phone out of his hand and threw it across the room with such force, that it collided with the wall, shattering into a dozen pieces. Edward looked completely dumbfounded and a little angry too. He opened his mouth to speak, but I never gave him the chance.

"If you want to work yourself to death, that's fine by me, but don't expect me to sit around and watch you do it!" I crossed my arms and turned my back to him, only to discover I was not the only person in the room. A group of older men in suits lined the opposite wall of the room from Edward's bed. I knew these men. They were members of the board of directors for Chesapeake Biotech, the company that Edward had been the CEO of for over a dozen years. After Edward had me attend a board meeting in January, I affectionately nicknamed these men "The Suits".

"What are y'all doing in here? Did you *not* get the memo? Edward had a heart attack two days ago. He will not be conducting any business from this room."

"But, ma'am," one of the men said. "He called us here."

"Well, I'm *un-calling* you. Out! All of you! Now!" The men looked at me and then Edward. I don't know what he did, but all the men dispersed and apologized to me as they did so.

I then turned my focus to Kelly. She was sitting next to Edward in the recliner and when our eyes met, she knew she was in hot water and diverted her eyes to the floor.

"And you! You should know better. I don't care who you work for, this is not one of those times you say yes to everything my husband wants. Just remember, if he dies, there won't be anyone around to sign your paychecks!"

Edward waited a long moment before speaking, still trying to curb his own temper. "Cassandra, I'm the CEO of a major corporation. Business doesn't come to a halt just because I'm in the hospital."

"You didn't get the memo either, huh?!" I turned around so I could stare him down. As I did, I moved closer to him, one loud step at a time. "You almost died. I don't give a damn about Chesapeake Biotech or even Thomas Hall for that matter! I need you to listen to what the doctors tell you to do and actually do it!" At this point, my face was mere inches away from his. "You are no good to me or our baby if you're dead!"

It took me a moment to realize I was yelling and had just dropped the baby news in Edward's lap. I pulled back and before I turned around saw Edward's smiling face. I pivoted and started to stomp out of the room, digging my heels into the linoleum as I went. Just outside the door, a group of nurses and Edward's doctor had formed to see what the commotion was about. When I reached them, they parted like the Red Sea and made a path for me as I continued down the hall toward the elevator.

Angry tears were already rolling down my face when I walked out the front entrance of the hospital and into a wall of cameras and questions. I stared aimlessly at the reporters that had set up camp. I silently turned and walked back into the lobby.

I had only taken one or two steps when I heard a familiar voice.

"Cassandra? Are you okay?" I looked to my left only to see Henry walking towards me, having just entered the building. His eyes were full of concern. The look on my face must have spoken volumes. "Where do you want to go? It's obvious you need a break."

"Somewhere with fresh air, but not out there." I pointed toward the door. "Key West maybe?"

Henry smiled and it helped somehow. He took my hand and lead me toward the first member of the hospital staff he could find. She was one of the floor nurses where Edward was currently a patient. She was petite and thin. She always wore her bleached, blonde hair in a severe bun low on her head. I did not hear what Henry said to her, but her eyes kept returning to my hand in his. She did not know how we were related and I was certain this would make its way into the tabloids. I only heard the last bit of his request.

"... So, she just needs someplace quiet outside for a few minutes, away from the press."

"There's a little courtyard that might work. Follow me."

We walked down a hall, through a door labeled Authorized Personnel Only, down another hall, and out the door at the end of it. She swiped her card key and held the door open for us as we walked into the daylight. I stopped when I reached her and read her nametag.

"Thank you, Nurse Hines. I appreciate everything..." but I could not find the words to finish the sentence. These incredible people were waiting on my husband hand and foot while monitoring his every vital sign. Thank you just did not seem like enough. Her response was that of pure grace.

"My pleasure," she said, staring at our hands again.

"He's one of my brothers-in-law, nothing more."

"You're lucky to have family that cares for you." She looked at her watch. "I've got to go. Stay as long as you'd like."

The nurse closed the door behind her and was gone. Somehow, I doubted I would see anything about this in the papers. As we spoke, she had given off an air of sincerity.

If you didn't know there was a courtyard there, it would be easy to assume you were walking into another room. I had no idea why this oasis was here, but I was thankful for it.

The courtyard was small but well maintained. The flowers were all in full bloom and park benches were scattered around a pebbled path that encircled a small, well-manicured, willow tree. The moment I saw the tree, I thought about our tree at Thomas Hall. This willow was much smaller but just as beautiful. As I thought, every tear I had tried to hold back over the last few days, every frustration, every fear, swelled from my body as a flood poured from my eyes. I crumbled into one of the benches and curled up into a ball, wrapping my arms around my drawn-up legs with my chin resting on my knees. Henry sat next to me and handed me his handkerchief when I was done. I dried my eyes, unwrapped my arms from my legs, and sat up.

"Feeling any better?"

"I don't know. It's all just too much." I heard the words I said and had a personal epiphany. This is what I said before every nervous breakdown I experienced. Knowing I had just said this terrified me. I could not let myself break down. Not now. Too much was at stake. It was no longer only about me. It was no longer about the two of us either.

When my cell phone rang, I checked the caller ID. It was Kelly.

"Kelly, I know my husband is domineering, but you can't let him do things like hold meetings in a hospital room."

"So, I'm domineering?" It was not Kelly. My husband confiscated her phone.

I did not say a word and my jaw muscles tightened.

"Are you okay?" I knew he was not angry but truly concerned about me. However, if I tried to have a conversation with him, I was certain I would start yelling again.

"I can't talk to you right now. Please don't call me again." I hung up the phone and it immediately started ringing again. It was Kelly's number. Edward no doubt. I declined the call.

I sat staring at Henry. So many things were going through my head. As angry as I was with my husband, I was worried.

"Henry, what if—"

He cut me off. "Don't go there. He's doing better today. Try to focus on one day at a time."

"Would that focus include me going psycho on my husband like I did a few minutes ago? I just threw Edward's cell phone against the wall of his hospital room and kicked the board members out."

Henry tried to hold it in, but couldn't and his laughter escaped in quiet snorts. "Excuse me?"

"You heard me." I took a deep breath and stared up into a clear blue sky.

"Cassandra, you are the strongest, smartest, most resilient woman I've ever met. Everything is going to be fine. Just don't bottle things up. Whether you'll admit it or not, you're under a lot of stress right now." As we spoke, I heard his cell phone vibrate. He stood and fished it out of his pocket.

"Hello. Yes, what can I do for you?" Henry smiled, raised his eyebrows, and then gave me a quick wink. I knew who was on the other end of the line. "I wouldn't worry too much. Edward, quit yelling. She's right here and she's fine. She hasn't even left the hospital. Wait a minute! She's what?"

"And tell him I'm still mad. And that he's being stupid. And I'll be the one raising this baby all alone! And it will be all his fault!"

"You heard that? Good, because I didn't want to have to repeat it to you. Okay. No problem. Bye." He was still standing when he hung up the phone. "No wonder you look exhausted. How far along are you, Sis?"

"About ten or eleven weeks. I could not have picked a worse time to finally get pregnant, could I? Between the vineyard sabotage, Edward's heart attack, and Poppy's death, this is definitely not the most stress-free time to be doing this."

Henry smiled and gave me a hug once I stood. We stood silent for what seemed like a long time. Henry gave great bear hugs that swallowed people in his love and affection. He always knew when I needed one. "Why don't you go home and get some sleep? You'll feel better once you have."

Home. I knew he meant the hotel suite Vivian had arranged, but I wanted to be at Thomas Hall. And that was exactly where I was going. Edward did not need me at the hospital tonight. There were plenty of nurses who could look after him.

Chapter Twenty-Six

I slept in the back of Edward's limo during the hour trip home. When the driver dropped me at the door of our house, I opened the car door myself, stood up into the daylight, and smiled just a little. I thanked the driver and then wasted no time walking into the house. As I did, my phone rang. The caller ID said Vivian. I knew it was probably Edward but I was not going to risk being disrespectful to my mother-in-law.

"Cassandra, please don't hang up. I just want to know that you're okay." I was right. It was Edward. Again.

"I'm fine." I kept my voice monotone.

"Come back to my room, Sweetie."

"I'm at Thomas Hall. I'll talk to you in the morning."

I hung up before Edward could respond and then quickly changed into shorts and a tank top, pulling my hair into a ponytail, and slipping on my favorite flip flops. The clothes, which were usually loose, felt tight and uncomfortable. However, I did not bother changing into something different.

I walked down the familiar path, passing Henry's house along the way. When I arrived at the production building, I stopped and looked at the oversized warehouse. How had such a generic-looking building changed my life? Its gray aluminum siding and industrial box shape was nothing extraordinary to gaze upon as it stuck out in contrast to the brick buildings and homes on the property. However, it was one of my favorite places to see. As I looked, Alex and Libby-Mae walked out, heading home. I didn't realize it was so late in the day.

Within a second, Alex was standing next to me having raced to lessen the distance between us. "Cassandra, what are you doing here? Is Edward alright?"

"Yeah, He's going to be fine. I just had to get out of D.C. for the night. I thought I'd check my messages while I was here."

"Well, there's nothing to check," Libby-Mae said, now having caught back up to Alex. "Alex and I have handled everything. The only thing on your desk is a list of people who called to wish Edward a speedy recovery."

"Hmm. Maybe Vivian's right. Maybe I don't need to be spending so much time at the office." Vivian reminded me often that Thomas Hall Winery had been a hobby for her late husband, Senior, and was never meant to be a full-time job. However, I quickly turned it into one.

"No. I don't think so!" Alex was quick to interject. "I don't know how you do it. Juggling all these little details at once. It gives me a headache. Feel free to come back soon."

"It won't be much longer, I promise." I stared at the building again and then the path that led up to the main house. "I guess, I'll just go find some dinner then."

"Did you want to join us? We were going to run into town and grab a bite at the diner." I looked at the two of them together, now holding hands. When had they become a couple? It seemed so obvious, and yet, I somehow managed to miss it. I knew Alex had been infatuated with Libby-Mae since the day she started working at Thomas Hall, but at some point, in the last six months, their friendship had become something more. My stare lingered on their hands a moment longer before looking up at them.

"When did this happen?"

"Valentine's Day," Libby-Mae said sheepishly as she blushed.

"That long ago? Are you trying to keep this a secret?"

"Yeah, from you," Alex said. "Everyone else knows. Including your husband. After the conversation we had before your wedding, I knew you wouldn't be happy about it."

I let out a deep sigh. "I told you my reasons, but you're both adults. As long as you're happy and it doesn't mess with the winery's harmony, I really can't object."

They both loudly exhaled and simultaneously looked relieved.

"Are you coming with us?" Alex asked.

"No, you two go ahead. I'm just going to go raid the kitchen and then try to get some sleep."

As I made my way to the main house, I had a different thought. I pulled out my phone and dialed.

"Hey, Brian."

"Cassandra, I am so, so sorry. I don't know what else to say."

"Nothing. I should be apologizing to you. I shouldn't have walked out of your office Tuesday. I should have stayed and given us an opportunity to talk about everything."

"Cassandra, I can't believe you think you need to apologize to me."

"We're friends now. I guess it really doesn't matter how we started. What are you and the girls doing for dinner tonight? We could do tacos and the girls could go for a swim."

"That sounds great except the girls are at a sleepover."

"Well, in that case, pick up tacos from the Mexican restaurant on your way here. I'm not going to do a whole taco bar just for the two of us."

"Am I a delivery service now?"

"You are tonight," I said laughing.

We finished our phone conversation just in time for my cell to ring again. It was Edward. Kelly had replaced his phone. I let it go to voicemail. A few seconds later, the texts began.

I'm sorry I upset you. You were right. I should be focusing on my recovery. I love you.

I stared at the phone for a few minutes before replying.

I love you too.

I had never typed those words out before. It felt a little weird.

I'm tired. I'm going to eat and make an early night of it. I'll see you in the morning.

I intentionally did not tell him I was having dinner with Brian. He did not need to know everything I was doing. It was my decision, not his. I had decided long ago that only I would control my life. I had only been semi-successful in doing so. I planned to change that.

Brian arrived within the hour with tacos, rice, refried beans, and ice cream. We sat on the back patio, ate, and caught up on all the happenings of the week.

"I looked over all the vine poisoning evidence again this morning," Brian commented as we finished off the ice cream he brought. "There's a pattern to it."

"Wait, what? That's not what I thought you'd say. How did I not see it?"

"You've been a little busy between mob hits and heart attacks. Speaking of, my condolences. I know you and Poppy were close."

"Thank you. I appreciate it."

"How's Edward recovering?" He tried to sound sincere with his inquiry. It was not very convincing.

"Fine, if I don't kill him before he's discharged from the hospital. I had a bit of a temper tantrum at the hospital today. But enough about my chaotic life. Tell me about the pattern."

"Best I can tell, whoever is doing this is doing it the same day or night of the week." I thought about what Brian said. Late April was the first attack on the vines. They had already been dead a week when we found them. That would put the poisoning on a Thursday or Friday. The second time, the dying vines were found on a Monday, but had been dead for only a few days. Once again, that means the day of destruction was Friday or Saturday. Just this

Monday, more dead vines were found. Counting backwards it had to be done on Friday.

"Fridays. Tomorrow is Friday. Any thoughts on how to handle it? I can't let this happen again, Brian. The winery won't survive it."

He only stayed a couple of hours, but by the time he left, our friendship was back on track and there was a plan in place for tomorrow night. The only thing was, I didn't tell him I was pregnant. I'm not sure why though. It seemed I was not telling anyone. Of course, after my outburst in the hospital, I was certain the word was rapidly spreading around Washington D.C. I figured everyone else would know soon enough.

When the sun rose the next morning, I found myself in the bathroom heaving. As I lay across the cool marble tiles of the floor, I realized that I had been having pregnancy symptoms for weeks and did not even realize it. I knew one thing already though; morning sickness was no joke.

I intended on being in D.C. before breakfast, but it was nearly ten when I quietly walked into Edward's room. He was wearing khaki pants and a light blue button-down collared shirt, sitting in the recliner meant for visitors and reading the newspaper. He peeked over the top edge of the paper to see who had arrived and then immediately removed his glasses, folded the paper, and put it on the floor next to him.

"Come here, Sweetie," he said, grinning from ear to ear.

I walked over to him and hesitantly sat on his lap, then immediately wove my fingers into the hair on the nape of his neck. "I'm sorry about yesterday. I..., I..., I don't know. I just lost it and everything I was thinking poured out of me. I feel terrible about how I talked to Kelly too."

"Kelly's fine. After you left, she told me that all of it was definitely the pregnancy hormones talking."

I felt my bottom lips quiver. So far, being pregnant sucked.

"I'm okay too. Really."

"It wasn't the way I wanted to tell you about the baby either."

"Well, it was memorable," Edward continued smiling and then kissed the bare shoulder exposed by my sundress as he rested one hand on my stomach. He waited for me to smile before continuing. "But to be honest, I was beginning to wonder if you were pregnant. You've been sick, exhausted, a little emotional, and I'm certain that you have missed at least one period. How far along?"

"About ten weeks. Maybe a little more."

"Ten weeks! You're almost done with the first trimester. How long have you known?"

"I started to suspect that I was pregnant a couple of weeks ago, but I wasn't certain until I was in Chicago. When I was at the hospital, I requested a pregnancy test when they offered me a prescription for pain meds."

"Cassie, that was a week ago. Any reason why I'm just finding out?"

"For some reason, I was shocked. I know we've been trying, but I just couldn't wrap my head around it. Let alone say it out loud." He simply smiled and continued with his happy litany of questions.

"Who else knows? Can I tell people?"

"You, me, Henry, anyone who heard me yell at you, and whoever's phones you borrowed." I gave Edward a sheepish grin. "And yes, I think it's safe for you to tell anyone you want."

"What's wrong? Your face has terror written all over it." Edward cupped one hand against my cheek and I leaned into it.

"My face is a pretty good indicator of how I'm feeling at the moment. I've always known I wanted to be a mother, but I never really thought about the whole pregnancy part of it. I don't know anything about being pregnant or giving birth. I know women have been doing this for thousands of years, but I don't know how to do this!" These were the moments I needed my mom and wished she and my dad were still alive.

Edward softly brushed his lips against mine before speaking, his fingertips gently holding my chin. "So do what you do best, Sweetie. Read. Learn. Go to the bookstore before they discharge me this afternoon and buy out the pregnancy and parenting section."

"I was wondering why you were dressed. I get to take you home today?"

"That's the plan. Speaking of plans, I want to talk to an architect soon about adding on to the house."

"The house is fine. It has two bedrooms. When guests come, we'll just put them at the main house."

"I like having a guest room and I know you want a big family so this won't be our only child. We'll need rooms for them all and a place for the nanny, and a playroom. I should probably put in a proper office too."

"If we do that, we may as well just build a whole new house," I said sarcastically.

"That's not a bad idea. I should talk to Mom about the land and location." My sarcasm fell on deaf ears. He was absolutely serious.

Building a new house and a baby simultaneously seemed like a very bad idea. But after a little consideration, we were going to need more space eventually. We may as well do it soon if we were going to do it at all.

Chapter Twenty-Seven

"THIS IS TERRIFYING, EDWARD!" My eyes were still the size of saucers when I set down my shiny new copy of *What to Expect When You're Expecting* on the coffee table. "How in the world am I supposed to do this?"

Edward stood up from the chair he was reading in and relocated himself to the sofa with me. His Cheshire cat grin was plastered on his face. It had been that way ever since he was discharged from the hospital. I wasn't smiling at all. The books on pregnancy that were meant to reassure me were having the opposite effect.

"Cassie, Sweetie, I think you're a little overwhelmed. Trying to read all of this at once might not be the best approach. Maybe no more reading for today." He slid the pile of books on the table out of my reach.

"Maybe no more reading, ever." I could hear myself sounding whiny and pouty as I spoke. I hated it but could not seem to control it.

Edward laughed as he leaned in and kissed the quickly fading scar on my temple while he pulled me close to him. The hospital bracelet was still on him when he wrapped his arms around me. We had only been home a couple of hours but I wanted that reminder of the last few days off of him. I unwrapped myself from him, walked over to the desk, and grabbed a pair of scissors. I walked back, made quick work of my mission, and re-wrapped myself in my husband's arms.

"Just remember, *we* are having a baby, not *you*. You're not alone."

"Yes, but *you* don't have to give birth. I don't think I can do this," My eyes filled with tears. When he looked at me, Edward knew there was nothing he could say that would extinguish the fear.

"Okay, I think we need some backup here. Let's call Zoe."

"Edward, how is Zoe going to help? She's childless."

His eyes squinted and he tilted his head to one side. "She's never told you? She raised a son."

Edward picked up the phone and dialed Zoe's number. While he spoke to her, I called Vivian. I wanted her to hear the news from me. As soon as she picked up the phone, I realized she probably already knew as Edward had borrowed her phone in the hospital to check on me. I blurted out everything in one breath. "Vivian, I'm pregnant, terrified, and beginning to think this was a bad idea."

She could not contain her joy as she giggled into the phone. "Cassandra, take a moment to breathe. It's going to be fine. Try to stay calm." I had been calm until I told Edward. Once I said the words 'baby' and 'pregnant' out loud to him, panic had become my default emotion. I followed Vivian's advice and took a few deep breaths.

"Okay, now what do I do?"

"Just enjoy being pregnant for a while. We'll plan a shopping trip soon. Eventually, your clothes aren't going to fit and something will need to be specially made for the Harvest Ball."

"I'm already there. None of my shorts are comfortable. And this morning it feels like all of my bras are two sizes too small." I hadn't even thought about the ball. I would be huge by then.

"Cassandra, how far along are you?"

"About ten weeks. Maybe a little more. I've got a doctor's appointment the week after next. I'll know more then." There was silence on the other end of the line. "Vivian?"

"I'm here."

"What are you thinking? You're very quiet all of the sudden."

"Your clothes aren't fitting already, you're only ten weeks pregnant, and it's your first child. I'm sure you're aware that twins run in my family." I could not make any sound come out of my mouth. "Cassandra?"

"Uh-huh." I finally managed to mumble. "I've got to go." I had not said hello and I didn't say goodbye either. I just ended the call and sat, dazed and terrified at the possibility of twins.

I looked at Edward with his beautiful brown eyes staring back at me and smiled. Maybe our child will have his father's eyes. "I just talked to Zoe. She and Henry are going to come over for lunch on Sunday. I think you will find her very reassuring."

"I think I need to lie down for a bit. Come rest with me. The doctor said you should rest."

"I think that's an excellent idea. You need lots of rest too. Our daughter is going to need that energy to grow."

"You mean our son," I replied as we climbed into bed.

"Definitely a girl," he argued playfully as he wrapped his arms around me, his hands protectively resting on my stomach. As soon as I felt his hands there, for the first time in days, I felt calm and relaxed.

Edward fell asleep early for the night, which made my job easier. I crawled out of bed around nine, squeezed into black shorts and a black t-shirt, laced up my tennis shoes, and walked over to the production building. When I arrived, Henry, Alex, Libby-Mae, Brian, and half of the Willow Creek police force were waiting for me. They had all been briefed on the plan. Patrol every row of grapes until sunrise. Everyone was assigned to specific fields.

Edward and Vivian were not to be disturbed under any circumstances. Vivian never acted elderly but she was well into her seventies and did not need to be involved. As for Edward, he was in no shape to physically be out in the fields but would push himself if he knew. In addition, he would absolutely forbid me from this mission. It was going to be a long pregnancy. He was always overprotective of me but I could tell he planned on taking it to a new level. What I did not know was that he already had an unexpected ally.

Originally, I had been assigned three fields, but it had magically been reduced to zero. I marched over to Brian squinty-eyed and seething. "What's this? Where are my fields?"

"Change of plans. I brought too many people and I don't like the idea of you being out there in your condition. You should have told me, Cassandra. I had to hear it from Henry earlier today. I promised him I wouldn't let you do anything risky. So, you're staying here."

There was no doubt in my mind that Edward had spoken to his brothers in regard to keeping me out of danger during this pregnancy and Henry had passed this on to Brian.

"Channeling your inner Edward now?" I knew my comment regarding his over-protectiveness stung deep, switching his mood from happy to agitated in a heartbeat.

"You know that's an insult in my book, right?"

"Why do you think I said it?" The question came out sounding more indignant than I had intended.

Brian snorted, let out a laugh, and shook his head. "Are you going to be this snarky until you have the baby?"

"Hmm," I grumbled. "I'm not going to stand around doing nothing all night."

"Why don't you get some rest? I'll call you if we find something."

"I'm not going to bed! I'm pregnant, not an invalid. I'll go find something to do." And with that, I turned in a huff and walked away.

With no fields to check, I decided to look around the production building in search of any signs of foul play. If someone could get through the fence, guards, and gate, they could get in the building. Everything looked as it always did until I reached the door to the cellar. It was ajar. The door was never open, even when people were working in the cellar, stacking bottles or filling orders, the door remained shut.

I picked up a flashlight from the bin by the door, turned it on, flipped the light switch, and made my way down the steps. Even with all of the lights on, parts of the cellar were pitch black. I slowly walked down the main corridor of the sprawling cavernous area until I reached another set of steps. I knew these well. They led up to the main house. Turning back around, I moved slowly, shining the flashlight into the darkened rows on each side of me. I was about halfway back when I saw two boxes pushed haphazardly off to one side, exposing a wooden door at the end of a row. Vivian, who gave me my first tour of the cellar, told me how this had been used to smuggle slaves to freedom during the Civil War. However, all the tunnels had been sealed at the end of Prohibition as they were no longer needed.

I made my way to the door and struggled against the rusted hinges. The other side was a tunnel four feet tall by four feet wide. The walls were dirt, as was the floor, but everything was reinforced with wooden beams. I dropped to my hands and knees. The tunnel was creepy. The damp and dusty air was suffocating. As I crawled, I began to wonder if this was a smart idea. I was in an old tunnel, with an unknown way out, if there was a way at all, and I was pregnant. It did not stop me though. As I made my way through the tunnel, I spotted something white on the ground ahead of me when the light from my flashlight hit it. As I moved closer, my first thought was that it was small, crumbled pieces of paper. Soon enough though, everything came into clear focus. Three discolored cigarette butts littered the ground. They were not relics, but relatively new.

I crawled for what seemed like the length of a football field before I saw an opening overhead just before the end of the tunnel. I stood up and looked around to find myself on the outside of the fence that encased Thomas Hall. Pulling myself from the hole, I found myself standing on a thick piece of plywood. I assumed it was to cover the hole when not in use.

As I stood brushing the dirt and mud off myself and inhaling fresh air, a bright light obscured my ability to see.

"Cassandra?" I knew the baritone voice well.

"It's me, Brian. I just found the security breach." Brian moved his flashlight so he was no longer blinding me. After quick directions for Brian as to how I got to where I was, I found him climbing out of the same hole I ascended from just outside of the fence line.

"This is amazing! It definitely explains how someone has been getting past the guard gate. I already bagged up the cigarette butts as evidence. I doubt anything will come back from the lab, but it never hurts to try." Brian fished his cell phone from his pocket and dialed. As soon as the call was answered, he put it on speakerphone so I could listen in as well. "Bubba, we found something you should see."

It took about ten minutes before both Brick and Bubba arrived in a Jeep. Thaddeus "Brick" Jones was the shorter of the two men at six foot four and the total weight of he and Bubba combined was just under six hundred pounds. It was difficult to tell if the weight was from muscle or fat as they always wore dark suits, white dress shirts, and black ties. The two had opted not to crawl through the tunnel. If I were them, I would not have either. Between their bulk, bad knees, and expensive clothes the tunnel was no place for them.

"Cassandra, who knew about these tunnels?" Brian questioned me as we made our way back through the tunnel toward the production room carefully examining it for any possible clues that we could have originally missed.

"I don't know. The fact they were dug to smuggle slaves to freedom during the Civil War is common knowledge, but I was told all of them were sealed after the end of Prohibition. I'm down in the cellar all the time and I didn't even notice the door to the tunnel. It had boxes stacked in front of it."

"I was beginning to think this vine destruction was an inside job, but now I have no idea. Anyone who knew about this tunnel could get into the winery. Do y'all have a security system for the production building?"

"We just lock it up at night. I always figured that was enough with the other security measures in place. A bunch of us have keys though."

"Anyone lose their keys recently?"

"Yes, actually. Me. I misplaced my work keys last month. Libby-Mae and I looked everywhere for them. We gave up and she made me a new set."

"Is it possible they were stolen?" Brian asked.

"Anything is possible, but I don't know how someone could take them. They are either in the bowl on my desk at home, the glass canister on my desk in the office, or in my pocket."

"You might want to look into having the production building and cellar locks rekeyed. Maybe set up a running list of who has key access as well."

"This has to be how the culprit is getting in and out of the building in the middle of the night."

"There's no doubt in my mind. Those cigarette butts looked fresh."

The sun was peeking over the horizon before I was in bed. It was Saturday morning and while I really wanted to sleep the day away, I was up before noon and was sorely disappointed no one showed up to get caught in the act and put this whole grapevine destruction to rest.

That evening, I listened while sitting at the kitchen table as Edward told my only living relative, Uncle Fred, that we were expecting. I was still struggling to say the words out loud to anyone but Edward. However, the news was spreading fast and I wanted him to hear it from one of us. As they wrapped up the call, I realized there were two very important people that needed to hear the news from me before they heard it through the Willow Creek gossip grapevine. These two would be easy to tell though. I picked up my cell from the desk in the living room and dialed.

"Hey, Gina. Is your sister with you?"

"Aunt Cassie! She sure is. You want me to put us both on speakerphone?" She didn't wait for an answer as she knew I would say yes.

"Hey girls. I need to ask you a question. How do y'all feel about babysitting? I'll be needing one or two babysitters eventually."

"You mean...?" They said in unison before squealing loud enough for Edward to walk out of the kitchen to investigate what was going on. When he realized who I was talking to, he smiled, shook his head, and went back into the kitchen.

"Now ladies, with the exception of Zoe, you are the first two people outside the winery to know."

"Actually, make that three," a baritone voice said that I knew was Brian's. I loved that he had not told the girls but waited for me to spring it on them. "Congratulations. I know you've wanted this for a while."

Chapter Twenty-Eight

Sunday afternoon, Edward and I sat in the living room as a thunderstorm pounded rain against the windows eating Chinese food and talking with Zoe and Henry. The two had been together for about seven months but were friends most of their lives. They were exact opposites and had almost nothing in common. And they were absolutely perfect for each other.

Zoe began telling me about her pregnancy when Henry interrupted her story.

"Are you sure you don't want something besides plain white rice and wonton soup?" Henry was concerned at how little I was eating. Chinese food sounded wonderful when we planned it the day before. But when it came time to eat, the scent of garlic hung in the air and my stomach felt like it was on a roller coaster.

"This is fine. If it stays down, maybe I'll get something more in a bit."

"Henry, quit pushing food on her. I hated when people did that," Zoe commented. "Edward, remember when you tried to do that?"

"Oh yeah. You vomited on one of my new suits. I think it was the only time I ever wore that one." They laughed and it suddenly occurred to me that there was something I did not know about my husband and brother-in-law. The curiosity must have shown on my face.

"Sweetie, what are you thinking about?" he asked with a smile.

"I'm sitting here wondering why you would wear a suit to school. What's the age difference between you and Henry?"

Henry interjected with the answer. "He's a decade older than I am, Cassandra. How did you not know that?"

"I don't know. I guess I've only ever seen you as you are now. Two grown men. I never really thought about you as kids or teens and what that looked like for y'all as brothers. I turned back to Zoe and said, "So, let me make sure I understand this. Your parents kicked you out of the house because you got pregnant?"

"Yep, my mother is a very traditional Asian parent. My parents wanted an A+ student, not a pregnant party girl."

"What about your dad?"

"You would have thought that my very American dad would have talked some sense into my mom. But that didn't happen. He's a man with no backbone. When I was a kid, I always thought he was the nice parent. When all of this played out, I watched as he did nothing. He never argued with her or offered to help me. He never did anything at all. He sent flowers to the hospital after I gave birth but I never heard from him again after that. My parents never met their grandson and they live ten minutes from my shop."

I shook my head and blew out a deep breath. How anyone could do that to their own child, I would never understand.

"Luckily, Henry and I were good friends. Mom kicked me out in the morning and by the time school was out that day, I had a home with Vivian and Senior at Thomas Hall. It was a crazy senior year of high school."

I was quickly discovering there was a lot I didn't know about the history of my circle of friends. My eyes went from Zoe to Henry and back to Zoe. "Was the baby's father Hen—"

"Oh, God no!" They shouted simultaneously, interrupting me. Once I stopped laughing, I continued my questioning.

"How long did you stay here?"

"Vivian refused to let me leave until after Max was born. About the time I was ready to leave, an apartment Edward owned became vacant. It's the one over the shop I live in now. I bought the building from Edward a few years back. The idiot probably didn't even charge me enough rent to cover utilities when we first moved in. It did make my life easier though."

I looked over at my husband. He was wearing blue jeans and a fitted gray t-shirt. Edward looked just as handsome in casual clothes as he did in a suit and tie. He was eating steamed chicken and vegetables with no sauce and pretending he wasn't listening to Zoe. I loved that man so much. He knew being a single, teenage mom would be hard for Zoe and did what he could to make things easier.

"Did you plan on going to cosmetology school by then?"

"I was halfway done when I had Max. It was one more thing my mom was mad about when she kicked me out. She wanted me to go to college." There was a sadness in her voice every time she said her son's name. A rock was forming in the pit of my stomach. I had a bad feeling this story wasn't going to have a happy ending. "The salon took off fast when I first opened it. The only other salon in town was an 'old lady' hair place. I drew in a younger crowd."

"Zoe, where's Max now?"

She closed her eyes and bowed her head. "I should probably finish that story. Max was a great kid." She said *was*. Sometimes I hated being right so often. "He grew up strong and smart. He would have loved you. You're not too much older than he would be now. Anyway, he decided to join the Marines after high school. I tried to talk him out of it. He was determined to do it. He did well at basic and ended up assigned to train for Delta Force."

I sighed. Now I definitely knew where this story was going, and it most certainly wasn't going to end with happily ever after. I decided to spare Zoe from having to finish the long version of the story. "How old was he?" I whispered.

She looked at me, saw my watery eyes and the single tear that had escaped, and knew I understood. "Nineteen. They couldn't tell me what happened. It's still classified. All they could tell me was that it was quick."

Henry reached his arm around her and hugged her tight. In my hormonal and over-emotional state, I had no words to comfort her. Zoe somehow found a smile though and said, "So, let's talk about this baby. I think you're going to have a girl."

"Thank you!" Edward said, finally fully joining the conversation. "Everybody keeps saying it's going to be a boy, but I'm certain they are wrong. But we'll find out next week at Cassie's doctor's appointment, right?"

I started to speak but Zoe beat me to it. "Edward, it's too soon. It will be at least another month and sometimes babies don't cooperate with the ultrasound equipment."

"Don't worry. My daughter will."

"You seem very certain of yourself, Mr. Baker. I guess," I hesitated but said it anyway as I smiled, "Time will tell."

Chapter Twenty-Nine

I DID NOT WANT to go back to Chicago. Not ever. Nevertheless, I found myself sitting on the private jet with Vivian early in the morning. Poppy's funeral was scheduled for just after lunch and I knew that I would regret not going.

Vivian and I decided to make the trip a single-day event. It would start early and end late. I did not want to leave Edward overnight. His heart attack haunted my thoughts and the less time we were apart the less stressed I felt. Vivian, as always, looked impeccable. Her hair was perfectly coiffed, her choice of black dress was perfect, and she even had a beautiful black, wide-brimmed hat. I, however, felt like a mess compared to her. I squeezed into a sleeveless black linen dress and my hair would not cooperate at all. I ended up pulling it back into a low ponytail. Vivian said I looked fine, but I'm fairly certain she was lying.

The car and driver I arranged for the day was waiting for us when we exited the plane. This had been a wise move for us. I could not imagine finding taxis that would take us where we needed to be in a timely fashion throughout the day. After escaping airport traffic, Vivian and I settled in for a quiet lunch at a small Italian bistro a block away from the church before the funeral.

We ordered our lunches and just after the waitress brought our drinks, I saw Mr. Gino Mantegna walking across the room toward us. There was little doubt in my mind that this was no accident. He was the man who took charge of my safety the night of the shooting and was doing the same now. I was certain he knew when our plane landed, who was driving the limo, and what route we would be traveling on. It was very reassuring.

The night we met, I had not paid too much attention to his looks or age. He was younger than I initially thought. About my age, or maybe a couple of years older, making him just shy of thirty. Very young for his position in the organization. I wondered for a brief moment how Poppy's death would affect his rank.

"Miss Cassandra. Mrs. Baker. I was not aware the two of you were acquainted."

"Vivian, is my mother-in-law."

Mr. Mantegna smiled before speaking. "I was unaware you had re-married, but it makes perfect sense. Both charming, beautiful women. Both living in Virginia. I won't keep you, but I wanted to wish you both my condolences."

"And mine to you as well sir," I replied.

"Not sir, just Gino." He pulled out two business cards and handed one to each of us. "Should you need anything, today or in the future, please do not hesitate to contact me. I made certain assurances to Mr. Scarpelli and intend to honor them."

Many conversations both before and after the funeral were carbon copies of the one we had with Gino. Condolences were exchanged, business cards handed to each of us, and some mention of promises that were made to Poppy concerning our well-being. While Vivian was the one with superb social skills, I was the one responding to the condolences. Vivian, for the most part, remained silent. At first, I thought it was part of her grieving process for Poppy, but as the day played out, I realized there was something more. As we sat in the car, en route to the reception after the funeral service and burial, I felt the need to comment on it.

"Vivian, you are very quiet today. If the reception is too much for you, we can skip it."

"I'll be fine, dear. I was not aware of how quiet I've been until you mentioned it. I've been thinking a lot about the last few days Poppy and I spent together. We were planning a trip. He wanted to take me to Italy. To the town where he was born. He was so excited." She gave me a sad smile. She turned and looked out the window as we passed through a neighborhood near Poppy's home. There was no way I was going to tell her he was trying to get her away from Chicago and the danger he felt he might be in. "The last time we spoke was the morning he died. He was so happy you were there and was looking forward to going to the theatre with you."

"Until the moment he died, he was happy that day. He'd had a good one. I'm just thankful the end was quick." I paused and let out a deep sigh before continuing. "I'm fairly certain he didn't know what happened to him. That's the way a true professional makes a hit. Clean and precise."

"I know you say you've stayed out of Poppy's business, but you know more than you realize. I've been watching you today. You know exactly how things work as well as what to say to whom and when. This world is alien to me. Poppy made sure I saw none of it and I know his reasons. I've really just been following your lead today."

I took a moment to contemplate her statement. Vivian was right. I did know more about Poppy's world than I would ever admit. As long as I could avoid a confrontation with Isabella at the reception, I would be able to continue the respectful condolences and meetings throughout the day. I was not certain I had the energy to deal with both a funeral and Izzy in the same afternoon.

Regardless, I tried to prepare myself for Izzy, but there's no way to prepare for a tornado like her. We had been at Poppy's house for about forty-five minutes when I saw her make her way across the room, anger plastered to her face. Vivian and I were standing next to Gino and they were having a conversation about wine.

"Gino, I'm sorry to interrupt, but would you please take Vivian somewhere besides here? Isabella is on her way over and I don't want her anywhere near my mother." This was a very bossy thing for me to say considering to whom I was speaking and the company in the room. Thankfully, Gino understood my concern without explanation. There was more at stake than he knew though. I knew that when, not if, Izzy accused me of murdering her brother that Vivian would try to convince her that she murdered Tony, not me. She did not need to spend the rest of her life looking over her shoulder, concerned about Izzy seeking revenge. Vivian and I were the only two people alive who knew exactly who was responsible for Tony's death and I was determined to keep it that way.

Vivian looked as though she were about to start asking questions, but Gino cut her off before the first word was spoken. "Mrs. Baker, follow me please."

They turned to walk away, and as they did, he turned back to me. "I'll send some people over."

As Izzy walked toward me, I contemplated our last meeting. She had startled me with her presence and frightened me in the process. I would not allow that to happen today. Luckily, the room was packed with witnesses.

"Isabella, I'm so sorry for your loss."

"Bitch, nobody wants you here!" I was about to offer to leave when one of Poppy's other granddaughters, Margaret, stepped between us. Margaret was older than both Izzy and me. Probably old enough to be my mother. Her grown children were not much younger than me. She was smart, quick-witted, rational, and had been operating parts of the organization for years. The perfect person to replace Poppy. Whether or not this traditional Italian family would allow a woman to run the family business had yet to be seen.

Before I could speak, Margaret chimed in.

"Cassandra will not be going anywhere. She has flown from Virginia to pay her respects to Poppy and the family and we will allow her to do so without incident." Margaret and I related to each other on several levels. She had been widowed when she was young. She spent time trying to rebuild her life afterward and was very involved in the family business. We did not see each other often, but when we did, we both felt the camaraderie that bonded us by our shared life experiences.

"Who died and left you in charge?" Izzy asked, crossing her arms in front of her and looking smug.

"Poppy did. Check the will. And if you think I'll keep letting you behave like this, think again, Bitch. Now, leave Cassandra and

Vivian alone and go harass someone else. I made assurances to Poppy and intend to uphold them."

"But she killed Tony! I want to see her suffer!"

Margaret began to speak but my voice escaped first and louder than I had intended. "Izzy, I'm going to say this one last time. I did not kill Tony. And if I had, you'd know it. Because, unlike you, I learned some things from Poppy. He taught me to own up to my actions, unlike your brother. I didn't fake my death and lie to my family! So, get out of my face because my patience is running thin."

It was only then I noticed there were no other voices in the room. Everyone had stopped talking and turned their attention to the two of us. Izzy said nothing. The shock on her face told an entire story. My story. I was no longer the mousy girl she could walk all over. And she did not like the new me at all.

Two men walked up to her and informed her they would be escorting her out of the room. Izzy planted her feet, crossed her arms in from of her chest, and stared me down. "This isn't over! Just you wait!"

When she refused to move, the two men lifted her so her feet were an inch off the ground and hauled her off, leaving Margaret and me to talk.

"Cassandra, it's been a while. You look fantastic and you have definitely grown a backbone since I saw you last." I had not noticed until that moment that she had Poppy's beautiful bright blue eyes. "You didn't really need me to tell her off. You definitely are capable of handling her yourself."

"Thanks," I said. "Margaret, a question, if you don't mind. You're like the eighth or ninth person today that's made a comment about assurances made to Poppy."

I never actually got to my question before Margaret answered it. "I think Poppy asked everyone loyal to him to protect you and Vivian. The two of you meant a lot to him."

"He asked me to look after Vivian, but I thought it was just because we're family." I could feel a wave of sadness roll over me. There was so much more I wish I could have said to Poppy.

"Wait, you two are family?"

"She's my mother-in-law. I introduced Poppy and Vivian to one another."

"You remarried?" She asked, looking surprised.

"Yes, this past Christmas. Poppy was at the wedding. It was a very small affair."

"Congratulations. I didn't know. I don't think anyone in the family does. Strange. I wonder why Poppy never mentioned it. All I knew was that he was going to Virginia a lot to see Vivian at some winery where she lived."

"Thomas Hall Winery. The winery I run. I live on the property as well."

"Is your husband here? I'd like to meet him."

"He, unfortunately, couldn't make the trip. He's recovering from a heart attack. He was fond of Poppy but the doctor said it was too soon for him to travel." All of this was true. However, I would not have let him come to the funeral regardless of his health. Chesapeake BioTech did not need to have any more of a connection to the Scarpelli Family crime organization than it already did. Whispers within Virginia's wine industry were starting to connect the family to Thomas Hall. After the day was over, and the dust settled, I would need to figure out a way to publicly put distance between the two entities. I was aware how optics could make or break a business and the winery could not afford another hit.

"Heart attack? How old is this new husband of yours?" Margaret asked.

"He's in his late forties," I said before pushing the conversation in a different direction. I knew Margaret would not comment on the age gap. It seemed to be a normal occurrence within the Scarpelli Family. Most marriages were arranged with the girl barely out of high school and the man in his late thirties. "Did Poppy really leave you in charge? I hope so. You are definitely the most qualified that I am aware of in the organization."

"Thanks for the vote of confidence." She reached into her bag and pulled out a business card and I did the same. "If you need anything, here's how to reach me."

"Same. I should probably let you get back to the other guests. I'm sure the next few weeks are going to be hectic."

She gave me a quick, friendly hug and a kiss on each cheek, much like a sister would, before walking away. I made a mental note to send her a case of wine. I had no desire to get mixed up with organized crime, but it never hurt to have the good favor of the woman in charge. She was going to need a friend and a drink or two in the very near future.

Chapter Thirty

FOR THE FIRST TIME in weeks, I was not exhausted. It seemed like ever since Bermuda I was consumed by sleep. It was only nine, on Friday night, but Edward had been fast asleep for over an hour. I encouraged him to get plenty of rest as I remembered my mom telling me once after a childhood injury that when you sleep, you heal. And that's exactly what Edward needed to do. I needed him well before this baby made his entrance into the world. I managed to escape the bed without waking him and got dressed. Well, I tried to. I discovered all the shorts I owned would no longer button. Even the pair I had worn the day before was so uncomfortable I couldn't stand to wear them. I finally gave up and threw a sundress over my head. My guess was it was going to be a summer of wearing sundresses. I found my favorite pair of Keds and grabbed my phone as I walked out the door and headed to the parking area of the production building where we all gathered last Friday evening.

While waiting for everyone to arrive, people milled about, conversing on a number of topics. I had not seen Brick or Bubba for the last two days and stopped to talk with them. As we began to converse, Alex and Libby-Mae joined us, hand-in-hand.

"Two of the new field lights went up today," Bubba said. "The rest will go up next week."

"Do you really think it will deter whoever is destroying the vines?" I asked.

"It can't hurt," Alex responded. "We probably should have done it sooner. I like the idea of being able to look out my back door and actually see the vines at night."

"How bright are these lights? Are they going to keep any of us awake?" I did not want anything to disturb Edward, not only that night, but any night. I found myself rubbing my barely pregnant belly.

Bubba gave a slight smile before responding. "Don't worry. We'll make sure the lights don't disturb the future little Baker."

I was just about to ask Bubba how he heard the news when Brian called for everyone's attention. "Okay, everybody. This is a repeat of last week. Everyone has the same field assignments. Let's hope we wrap this up tonight. Also, there are cold water bottles in the cooler. Stay hydrated."

Within minutes, everyone was where they were supposed to be. I was determined to walk the vines even though I was not assigned specific fields once again. I wanted to see the newly installed lights illuminate the fields. I had not been involved in the decision to install them. Bubba and Brick recommended to Alex they be put in while I was with Edward at the hospital in Washington D.C. and he approved it.

I walked across the path in front of our house, listening to the crickets in the humid night air before stepping straight into the first field. The lights gave a glow to the vines that reminded me of a streetlight. Bright in one spot and then dim all around the spot. I'm not certain what I expected, but this was not it. I wondered if I had misunderstood what the lights were intended to do. I used my phone as a flashlight to get a better view of the vines as I made my way up and down the rows. I saw an empty area, roped off, about halfway through this field. It was a spot where poisoned vines once called home. Knowing these attempts at sabotage could be the death of Thomas Hall Winery tormented me and I shook my head as I continued walking.

I finished the first field at a good pace and went on to the second field. There was no possible way that I was going to get through many fields tonight, but I could manage a few more. I was determined to find the person responsible for this destruction but I knew soon I would need to check in with Brian before calling it a night. Edward was asleep in our bed and I did not want him to wake and discover me not there. In addition, it was warmer than last Friday night and it left me feeling queasy.

I walked through dimly lit rows of vines until I heard a noise. I stopped, looked, and listened just in time for the sound to repeat itself. The distinct sound of pouring liquid was not far from where I was standing. I knew at that moment I should not be out in the fields alone. When I took my first step, my tennis shoe landed in a puddle, splashing, and possibly making my presence known. It was then the smell of gasoline invaded my senses. It was so strong it overpowered the scent of the grapevines and only increased my queasiness. As quietly as I could, I made my way to the end of the row to see what was happening.

When I turned the corner, I saw Stefanie with her back to me wearing cut-off jean shorts and a tank top. Her legs were dirty and my missing set of keys partially hung out of one of her back pockets. She was standing with a gas can in one hand and a gun in the other. I discreetly found Brian's number in my contacts, put it on speakerphone, and prayed for the best. It was luck the phone was already in my hand. If I had not been using the flashlight feature, I would have been unable to reach out for help so quickly. I watched as she poured more gasoline on the vines as the shadows from the vines obscured her face. My stomach twisted into a knot and my breathing became shallow but I said nothing until she set the gas can down and fished a lighter from her pocket.

"Stefanie! What on earth are you doing?" I asked and she jumped before quickly turning to face me.

"Oh, Jesus. Not you." She rolled her eyes as she continued to speak. "I thought you were supposed to be smart. What does it look like I'm doing? I'm about to torch as many of the vines as possible. Poisoning them was taking too long."

"That was you? Why?"

"Why? Because at the moment it's my job," she replied and set down the gas can. "I was hired to destroy both you and your winery."

I was at a loss as to who would want to destroy Thomas Hall. She raised the gun and aimed it at me, her hand steady and looking as though she wouldn't hesitate to pull the trigger. This was not the first time in the last year I found myself staring down the barrel of a gun. It's a feeling you never become comfortable with. Knowing that the bullet at the other end of the barrel can take your life and you have no control over it is unnerving. "I am pretty pissed that you're still alive. I thought I was done with you in Chicago. I don't remember the last time I missed a shot."

"Chicago? That was you?"

"So many people in jail are craving revenge and restitution. There's a lot of money to be made."

I was trying to think fast and formulate a plan but nothing came to mind. If I learned anything at all from the last time this happened to me, I knew I had to keep Stefanie talking. If your gunman is talking, they are distracted. "Did the same person who paid you to destroy me pay you to destroy my unborn child as well?"

"You're knocked up?" She laughed as she spoke. "Talk about history repeating itself. Who's the daddy? Brian or Edward?"

I rolled my eyes and quickly answered. "My husband is the father. I don't play men against each other like you do. Put the gun down, Stefanie." But she didn't. She kept the gun pointed at me as she dropped the unlit lighter and slid a cell phone out of her pocket. Stefanie's hands began to shake as she dialed a number, never moving her eyes from me.

"Hey, Izzy. It's Stef." Izzy was behind all of this? I was simultaneously dumbfounded but not surprised by this piece of breaking news. I watched as the shadows along the vines changed. Other people were close by. I was fairly certain they were part of Brian's team in the fields, but still found myself praying they were friends and not foes.

"Yeah, I'm doing it now. Problem though. That bitch Cassandra found me." She paused, and I could hear Izzy jabbering. "That was my first thought. Another opportunity to finish her off. But Izzy, she's pregnant."

I heard the smug tone of the response through the phone but couldn't tell what was said.

"You're kidding, right? If you want me to do that it's going to cost you a lot more." The other end of the phone now sounded like screeching cats, but I knew it was Izzy's shrill voice. "Fine, then come do it yourself." Stefanie threw the phone. It landed a row over from where we were standing with Izzy's voice still blaring out of it.

"God, that bitch's voice is annoying."

It was then half a dozen police officers came from all directions and I found Brian standing directly between me and Stefanie. She immediately dropped the weapon. I believe she realized at that moment she would never see her girls again and sadness overtook her smug expression.

I watched as Brian stared at Stefanie and was able to read his expression. She had a second chance to have a good life and she had blown it, again. Sadness reached Brian's eyes when he realized he was going to have to tell the twins that their mom was not going to be part of their lives. Georgie and Gina were going to be devastated, even if only one of them would admit it.

As another officer cuffed her, Brian turned in time to see me sway. The combination of shock and exhaustion was taking its toll. He grabbed me by the waist and held me steady. "Are you okay? I'm going to get a paramedic out here."

"Brian, I'm fine," I said, stepping back from him. "No one hurt me. I'm just tired. I don't need a paramedic. I need you to stop acting weird because I'm pregnant."

"Cut me some slack, okay? I just had to have the mother of my children arrested for trying to kill you. And your husband would have murdered me if anything happened to you out here."

"Fine. I'm really okay though. Just exhausted. So, did you hear everything or do you need me to go over what happened?"

"I heard. I'll come out tomorrow afternoon to get your official statement, so you can get some rest now. But Cassandra, who is Izzy?" He asked, all the while walking me back towards my home.

"Isabella Martin. You are not going to believe this, but she's Tony's sister."

"Oh, come on. Seriously? Tony's dead and he's still making trouble?"

I nodded and then I spoke, cutting him off from asking his next question. "And before you ask, the only thing I know that connects Stefanie and Izzy is that they both recently got out of prison."

I slid back into bed around two in the morning. Moonlight poured through the windows, giving me sufficient light to kick off my shoes and find my way between the soft sheets. I did not bother to change out of the sundress I was wearing. I really wanted to take a shower but knew the sound of the water would wake Edward. I snuggled up next to him and he wrapped his arms around me with his lips next to my ear.

"You've been gone a while," he whispered. "Everything okay?"

"It is. I just needed to handle something. I'll tell you all about it in the morning."

There was a pause long enough where I assumed he had fallen asleep.

"Did you catch the vine saboteur?" I had no clue how he figured out what I was up to and his statement surprised me. He knew this and continued. "I woke up about an hour ago. When I couldn't find you, I walked out to the pool and saw all the police cars parked along the path. It wasn't hard to figure out what was going on."

"I'm surprised you didn't run into the fields in a panic, searching for me."

"I wanted to, but I have to trust that the mother of my child knows what she's doing."

His statement gave me warm, fuzzy feelings. I was the mother of his child, wasn't I? And his lack of action proved he trusted my judgment, whether he should or not. I paused for a moment before returning to his original question. "Yes, we caught her. It was Stefanie. She's in custody. Go back to sleep."

"Yeah, I'm going to need more information about that in the morning." Edward kissed a sensitive spot behind my ear that made my whole body tingle and mere moments later he was asleep again. I followed about ten minutes later, sleeping peacefully with my husband's arms wrapped around me and his hands protecting our unborn child.

I felt Edward playing with my hair before I heard his voice. "Cassie, my love. I hate to wake you, but Brian is here to get your statement."

I pried one eye open and looked at the clock. It was one in the afternoon. I had slept eleven hours. The sound of the twins splashing around in the pool made me smile.

"When he called earlier, I told him to bring the twins for a swim."

"Good idea." I got up, pulled a purple sundress from my closet, and made my way to the bathroom. I only owned three sundresses. I would have to get Zoe to find some more. Twenty minutes later I was sitting next to the pool under an umbrella with an ice-cold glass of pineapple juice. I could always take or leave pineapple juice in the past, but in my pregnant state, I craved it.

While I gave my statement to Brian, Edward sat with me and listened. He was shocked to discover Isabella's involvement. Stefanie exposed everything Izzy was involved in and contracted her to do. In exchange for the information, Stefanie was offered a plea deal that did not involve the death penalty. Isabella Martin had hired and paid Stefanie Hayes to murder not only Poppy Scarpelli, but me as well. The two met when serving time in the same prison. When Izzy discovered that Stefanie was an expert shooter, she offered her a job upon her release as a hitwoman. The fact that I was connected to Edward and Brian was unknown to both Stefanie and Isabella when she agreed to the job. In Stefanie's opinion, my death was a bonus for her. It not only removed what she thought was a barrier between her and her girls but also would make Edward easily available for her to reunite with once I was dead. When she killed everyone in Chicago, Stefanie thought I was dead when I went to the ground and did not realize the fall was related to my fainting.

Izzy lawyered up and denied everything, of course. But I knew the motives behind her actions. Revenge and power. She wanted retribution for Tony's death and thought destroying the winery and murdering me was appropriate payback. In addition, she wanted to control the family business. The only way that could possibly happen was if Poppy was dead. She did not care if he was her grandfather or if he was responsible for getting her out of jail so quickly. She would not find the same quick release from prison this time. Margaret, who was now in charge of the organization, would be happy to leave her trouble-making cousin locked up.

By the time Brian was done with his report, the guys were dumbfounded as to the way my life once again played out. In less than a year, so much happened to me and all were things that hinged on the smallest detail.

Things like Edward's pilot getting the flu. If he had not, Edward would not have taken the commercial flight where we were seated together. It was our first meeting, even though our lives had many common threads.

Deciding to visit my friends after returning to the states just in time to answer a phone call when someone dialed the wrong number. That someone was Edward. This brought an invitation for me to Thomas Hall and the opportunity to reconnect with Edward.

Holding both of my late husband's death certificates, one fake and the other real, in my hand at the same time and realizing the same coroner was responsible for both of them. The coroner set a building on fire in an effort to silence me.

I knew that the last year of my life, plagued with death, destruction, and mayhem was not normal, even for me. Things would settle down and peace would return to the winery, at least for a while. However, nothing is perfect. Not even at Thomas Hall. Tragedy would still make the occasional appearance and the unexpected continued to be the norm for me. People would be born, and people would die. There would be happy days and sad days. There would be more secrets over the years too. Baker family secrets that I would carry to my grave.

Epilogue

TEN YEARS LATER

THE POOL WAS FULL of kids by eleven in the morning, even though the party did not officially start until noon. Everyone thought I was crazy hosting another Memorial Day Weekend pool party after the disastrous first one. Nevertheless, I kicked off every Summer with one. This one was extra special though. It was the tenth anniversary of the Baker Memorial Day Pool Party. It was almost as well known as the Harvest Ball and harder to get an invitation. I watched as my girls played Marco Polo with their younger cousins. It was a beautiful morning, but clouds rolling in from the southwest threatened rain before the day was out.

Edward was on the far side of the pool and I watched as he joined in the game. He was grinning and shaking his head as he responded to something Hope said to him. It reminded me of a different day a decade earlier.

I will always remember Edward grinning and shaking his head when we walked out of the obstetrician's office in Richmond and into the bright afternoon sun. I was stunned, nearly speechless. I had been wrong. So very wrong. I was not twelve weeks pregnant. After being examined by the doctor, she was insistent that an ultrasound be done to get a more accurate due date and examine the possibility of multiple babies.

"Sixteen weeks," was all I could say. And I did, over and over again. "Sixteen weeks. That means a Christmas baby. Maybe New Year's. Sixteen weeks."

"And a girl," Edward beamed as he stopped next to the car and embraced me. "The pictures are incredible!"

About halfway back to Thomas Hall, sitting in the back of the limo, I glanced at Edward, still staring at the ultrasound pictures. He was in love with this baby, and she hadn't even arrived yet.

I was pulled away from the memory when I heard Noah yell, "Sam! Grace! No running by the pool! You can run in the grass but I don't want any scraped-up knees from falling." He was nineteen now, devastatingly handsome like all the Baker men, and a lifeguard at the country club. He preferred working at parties for me though. I paid better and the commute was only walking across the backyard. Phoebe moved herself and the kids to Thomas Hall just before Noah started high school.

Sam and Grace continued to run about until Henry stopped them both. "What did Noah just say?"

"No running by the pool," the two said in unison.

"Listen to him or I'll have to take you home and we'll miss all the fun."

"Okay, Daddy!" No one was more surprised than Henry and Zoe when they discovered that Zoe was pregnant with twins on her forty-second birthday. The twins were about to graduate from kindergarten and thought they were as mature as their older cousins.

The year after Hope, our oldest, was born, Henry left Thomas Hall Winery. He bought an old warehouse in town and started The Baker's Dozen Brewing Company. Edward and I both agreed that we had never seen a business take off so quickly and become a financial success immediately.

"Doesn't it make you want to have another one?" Zoe asked me as we stretched out in lounge chairs. "You're in great shape and young enough. Any chance of a fourth child?"

"Three girls in three years was sufficient."

Once my body figured out how to get pregnant, it got very good at doing so. However, I would never have the boy I was certain I was pregnant with whenever I discovered I was expecting again. What Edward and I never told anyone was we wanted more children. But giving birth to so many children so quickly, one each December for three years in a row, took a toll on my body and my doctors advised against it. Plus, by the time Joy, our youngest child, was born, Edward was in his fifties. I wanted our children to have a father young enough to keep up with them. As I spoke, Hope hopped out of the pool and approached me.

"Mom, so I was just thinking, could I have a half-birthday party next month? We could use the pool and have a sleepover?"

"That sounds like fun but let's talk to Dad. Because you know if you have one your younger sisters will want to do the same and three half-birthday parties in one month is a lot."

"So, can we do it if Dad says yes?"

"Go talk to him." Hope skipped off in search of her father.

Zoe laughed and then took a sip of her soda. "So, three parties next month? You know Edward can't say no to the girls.

"Why do you think I sent her?" She laughed some more and I smiled. I watched as Hope pleaded her case to her father. She was being very serious and he was grinning from ear to ear. He turned and looked at me and I melted. After ten years of marriage, he still made me want to strip off all his clothes by just smiling at me. I didn't realize Zoe was watching the whole scene play out.

"He still really does it for you, doesn't he?"

"Yeah, and he always will. I'm certain of it." I scanned the yard and noticed one of my girls was nowhere to be found. I got up and went into the pool house, formerly the little home we lived in the first two years of our marriage.

Just as I suspected, Faith was sitting on the sofa, reading a book. She was the most like me. Especially when I was eight. I sat down next to her.

"What are you reading, Beautiful?"

"A book called Harry Potter and the Sorcerer's Stone."

"Great novel. If you like it, there's a whole series of them."

"I know. They're all in Gran's library." I smiled. I was beginning to believe Faith spent more time in Vivian's library than in her own room. However, there were worse places she could be spending her time.

"Mom, do you really think I'm beautiful?"

"Do I ever say something I don't mean?" Not only did we have similar personalities but she had many of my features. She wasn't built like her sisters. They were rail thin even though they ate like hippos, but she still had a little baby fat on her and at eight was already stressed about it. I hated that the girls at St. Margaret's

Academy teased her into having body issues. Well, they did until Joy reminded this group of mean girls that either her father or uncle signed most of their parents' paychecks so unless they liked being homeless, they better start being nice to her older sister.

"Of course, you're beautiful." A voice said from the sliding door. "You look just like your mother. But you know, you're missing the party. Stick a bookmark in that book and come on outside."

"Yes, Uncle Alex," she said with a smile. "I'm going to go to the bathroom first, though. I'll see you out there." Faith headed to the bathroom, and after she closed the door, I stood and turned to Alex.

"Thanks. It carries more credibility coming from her favorite uncle."

"She's so much like you. Beautiful and she doesn't even know it." I shyly smiled and headed back outside. Alex followed me and when we reached the pool, I found my husband splashing around with the kids.

I pulled my coverup over my head and tossed it on the table. I was wearing the same red bikini Zoe brought me the morning of our first Memorial Day party. Alex was quick to comment.

"Damn, still hot."

In my head, I flashed back to the day Alex kissed me, thinking I was interested in him. I wasn't. It was almost a decade ago and the thought still made me laugh. As I did, I lowered myself into the pool and found myself face to face with my husband.

"God, you are gorgeous!" Edward said loudly. "Is that the same bikini you wore the first Memorial Day you were at Thomas Hall?"

I nodded and he kissed me; slowly and softly until a quiet moan left my mouth. When he pulled his face away from mine, he stared at me before leaning back in and whispering in my ear.

"I really want to strip this bathing suit off of you right here, right now."

Before I could reply, Sam swam over to me and wrapped his arms around my neck in order to rest. "Aunt Cassie, why is your face all red?"

I looked at Edward and he just flashed me his famous Cheshire cat grin.

"I think my face is getting sunburnt. Swim over to your Uncle Edward and I'll go put on some extra sunscreen."

I applied more sunscreen, even though I knew that was not the real reason my face was red. As I did, Vivian arrived. She moved slower now than when we first met but was still as feisty as ever. She was in a white blouse and Khaki shorts looking fabulous as always.

"You look lovely today, my dear. And you're not sunburnt yet. It's a miracle."

"The day is still young."

As we spoke, Gina, Georgie, and Nora arrived. The girls had been inseparable for a couple of years and I did not want to even think about what they had been doing. The three ran a little wild and now they could all legally drink. Thank God they weren't my responsibility.

"Hello, ladies," Vivian said as a grin formed on her face. The troublemaking trio often called Vivian to get them out of trouble or even help in the planning of their adventures. She loved having the girls around.

"You won't believe what we did this morning," Georgie said, smiling.

"Stop there," I said. "Was it illegal? Because if it was, I don't want to know."

"Is breaking into Andrew Smith's house and emptying two cans of shaving cream in his bed illegal?" Nora asked. Vivian laughed at the question.

"The breaking and entering part is."

"Oh, then never mind," Gina said.

"Why did you do it?" Vivian asked.

"You don't cheat on Nora and get away with it," Georgie said.

I shook my head as the girls proceeded to where Libby-Mae sat to regale her with the morning's escapades in detail.

"I think I'm going to follow them. I want to hear the whole story," Vivian said before walking in their direction.

Brian, who arrived about twenty minutes before his girls, was about to open a beer to have with lunch when his phone rang. He answered and listened patiently as the caller spoke. When they were done, he paused for a second. "I'll handle it. Thanks for the call."

Once the call was over, he came over to me, looking exasperated. "The girls and I might have to leave early. It seems they broke into the Smith's home and vandalized it this morning while everyone was gone."

"You should let Phoebe know. Nora was with them. They have got to start thinking before they do these things. Henry and I have both told them that if they get arrested, the three of them are going to lose their jobs at the winery and brewery. We were hoping it would help keep them out of trouble." I shook my head. "They're adults now."

"I know, but they certainly don't act like it." He shook his head and rolled his eyes before he walked in the direction where Phoebe sat, eating her lunch, and enjoying a glass of wine.

I watched the huddle of girls listen to Vivian as she spoke to them. Alex was sitting next to Libby-Mae and burst out in laughter.

Alex and Libby-Mae married just after her twenty-first birthday. She moved in with him not long after Edward's heart attack. She decided to stay on at the winery full-time and attend college online. Libby-Mae majored in marketing and I attributed much of our success to her. She and Alex decided children were not part of their life plan. However, they were every child's favorite aunt and uncle.

Over the years. Alex made a name for himself as an innovative winemaster. Occasionally, other larger, more famous wineries would approach him about leaving Thomas Hall. He never even considered them. The winery was home for him as well.

I was blissfully happy watching everyone enjoy themselves. Edward walked over to me and handed me a glass of wine. It was a blended red Alex had insisted on bottling last season. I was initially opposed to it, but as usual, he was right. It was delicious. It seemed everything Alex touched turned to gold. It was because of him, not me, that the winery was thriving. For the last eight years, Thomas Hall turned a profit large enough that we were able to expand and open a joint tasting room with Henry in town.

Edward walked behind me and wrapped his free arm around my waist, pulling my back against the front of his torso before whispering in my ear, "Are you happy, Sweetie?"

I didn't turn to face him but reached back and played with the hair at the nape of his neck and I felt his lips trail down my neck.

"How could I not be? I mean, look at our family. Our world. It is absolutely wonderful." And at least at that moment, it was another perfect day.